Key Witch

Also by Robert Tacoma

Key Weird
Key Weirder

Key Witch

Robert Tacoma

Mango Press
Gainesville, Florida

For information address
Mango Press
P.O. Box 141261
Gainesville, FL 32614-1261
mangopress@gmail.com

This is a work of fiction. Names, characters, places, and
incidents either are products of the author's imagination or
are used fictitiously. Any resemblance to actual events or
locales or persons, living or dead, is entirely coincidental.

For information on books by Robert Tacoma:
www.tacobob.com
mangopress@gmail.com

Front cover illustration by Eva Everything.
Cover and interior design by Merrey Design.

First U.S. edition published 2006
Printed in the United States of America by Morris Publishing.

ISBN: 0-9760630-2-6

10 9 8 7 6 5 4 3 2 1

"Are you a good witch or a bad witch?"

"Oh, I'm not a witch at all! I'm Dorothy, from Kansas."

Chapter 1

Northern California

*As soon as the rain left, a heavy fog clocked
in for the late shift and went to work settling
in over the town of Pine Cove.*

Nestled in the center of the small historic section of town stood an old hotel that had seen a lot of foggy nights. But it wouldn't see many more. Not much time left for the towns-people to speculate whether or not the place was haunted or to gossip about the hotel's unusual proprietors. A shiny construction sign out front promised new things, coming soon.

The Majestic Hotel wasn't haunted, of course, though it did seem to loom a bit, its tall dark windows looking down on the street below. The few streetlights nearby seemed to produce more eerie shadows than guiding light.

Other than the occasional car skulking slowly along between the hotel and the brightly lit drugstore across the street, it was a quiet night. There was a little sniffing, sneaking, and shuffling going on along the fog-damp sidewalks as the wayward and homeless — dogs, cats, and people — did their best to slip by unnoticed on their late-night forays.

There were plenty of vacancies at the hotel, and the three young women sitting around a small table in the dimly lit, smoky office storeroom didn't expect any guests so late. The three were sisters, taking a night off. Some of the more gullible townsfolk believed any women who would run such a haunted-looking hotel must surely be witches. Never mind the absence of nose warts, pointed black hats, flying brooms, or cackling laughter. Well, maybe there was a little cackling, especially on poker night.

A single bare bulb hung from the ceiling above the poker table. Lydia shuffled cards for the first game of the evening while her sisters sat with their stacks of poker chips and snacks, watching her every move. She could shuffle cards like nobody's business, but then, that's to be expected when you're a magician. The oldest at twenty-one, with big brown eyes and very unwitchlike shoulder-length chestnut-brown hair, Lydia was a looker. But she paled in comparison to her younger sisters, whose concentration now focused totally on her delicate, perfectly manicured fingers. They relaxed only when she set the deck down for the cut.

"How about it, girls? Feeling lucky tonight?"

Consuelo, a year younger than Lydia, slipped the top third of the cards off the stack and placed them next to the pile. She was indeed prettier than her older sister, in a fresh, innocent, almost angelic kind of way. Not as tall, some might even say petite, with pixie-cut white-blonde hair and sparkling blue eyes. She was smoking a huge black cigar and blew a puff of smoke toward Lydia.

"Yep, as a matter of fact, I *am* feeling lucky tonight, Sis." Then she cut loose a long, loud belch.

"Jesus Christ, Consuelo! Could you possibly be any more gross?" Lydia leaned back and waved the smoke out of her eyes. "How about opening some windows! You're going to give us all lung cancer with that thing!"

Consuelo grudgingly got up. "Keep your hands away from those cards till I get back!"

She killed the beer she held in her hand and grabbed another out of the cooler on the floor next to her chair. "Keep an eye on her, Jos."

The third sister gave one quick nod of her head. Her determined look did not change, nor did she take her eyes off Lydia's hands. As usual, they didn't play for money, they played for a day off from the hotel they'd owned and operated for over a year since their mother passed away. It had been a tough time.

The sisters were older than their years. They'd had to grow up quick. There always seemed to be someone looking to take advantage of three girls in a crumbling old hotel with an ailing mother.

Consuelo opened a window and drew in a lungful. "Ah, Paris in the spring! Such a bouquet greets my hungry nose! A hearty base of car exhaust! The surprising strength of unwashed wino! The tangy top-note of dog poop!"

She brought more air to her nose with fluid motions of her muscular hand while looking back at her sisters. Lydia gave her a generous eye roll.

"Yes, dear. We're so happy you've discovered *Dollars and Scents* on television."

Consuelo shrugged and puffed on her cigar as she walked back to the table. Lydia selected another chocolate cookie out of her bag of treats lying next to the cards. Despite her strength, Consuelo envied her talented sisters and could never resist the chance at a dig.

"Hitting the choc pretty hard tonight, Sis. You still upset about Barry?"

Lydia slowly guided the cookie toward her mouth with only one finger, her middle finger, and it was aimed at her taunting little sister.

"It was mutual. We decided we needed to see other people so our relationship could mature."

Her two younger sisters burst into laughter. Despite her maturity and street-smarts, Lydia had a well-known history of falling for the absolutely wrong guy and getting hurt. Barry turned out to be not only a total jerk but married. The surprising and embarrassing married thing was revealed by Barry's cousin, who ran a detailed and unflattering account of the break-up in the society column of the local newspaper.

But the laughter stopped abruptly when Lydia's hands touched the deck of cards.

"Five card draw, ladies. Death, the Devil, and Deuces are wild. Bet heavy, and don't be shy."

They studied their cards with keen concentration. As usual, they used a tarot deck to play poker. It made it a little more interesting. Never knew when you might get a royal flush, or find out you were going to be lucky in love, or come into some money, or die.

Lydia peeked over her cards at her youngest sister. Talk about looking like a witch. With big dark eyes and raven hair, Josephine bore a strong resemblance to Elvira. At nineteen, she'd filled out to a stunning likeness of the Mistress of the Dark.

Lydia was trying to read Josephine's poker face when Consuelo cracked her knuckles and set some cards face down on the table. The lithesome blonde tended to be just as perky and cheerful as she looked, but her hands were shocking if you looked close. They were not just muscular, but scarred and calloused from years of martial arts training. As part of her next long beer belch Consuelo said, "Three."

"The little lady with the manners of a pig takes three." Lydia flipped three cards out so fast they looked like one. "How about you, Princess Bug-breath, any cards?"

Josephine could speak, but not very well. She had a heartbreaking stutter, especially when she was excited, which was most of the time. Despite her beauty, Josephine didn't have many boyfriends. Part of it was the stuttering, but it was mostly due to her unique talent for identifying edible insects and then eating them on the spot. That kind of news spread quickly in a small town. She smiled sweetly and held up fingers for two cards in a way that looked suspiciously close to the British gesture for sticking it.

"And two cards for our demure little entomologist. Dealer takes one." Only after Lydia placed the remainder of the deck on the table did her two sisters finally take their eyes off her hands and look at their own cards.

Consuelo looked confident.

"Open with a fiver." She tossed a chip on the table.

"You know, Barry may be dumb as a rock, but at least he's real." She shot her younger sister a look. Josephine ignored the dig and didn't even glance up from her cards as she dropped a five-dollar chip on the table, then another. The dark-haired beauty had gardener's hands. Though they were slender and delicate, there was usually a dirty fingernail or two.

"C-call f-five and raise f-f-five."

Consuelo kept at it. "At least Barry's got something for a woman, unlike Josey's little *Ben.*"

Josephine slapped her cards face-down on the table the same instant as Consuelo. Both women stared at each other with pure white-hot hatred filling their eyes. Lydia calmly slipped two aces out from under the cookie bag and into her hand. She concentrated on arranging her cards and ignored the stare-down going on between her two snarling, teeth-baring siblings.

Consuelo started to waver and looked as though she might lose consciousness. Lydia was about to say something when Consuelo broke it off by looking down. As soon as she did, Josephine smiled a satisfied smile and picked up her cards. Consuelo looked dazed. Her cigar had gone out, so she carefully put it in the ashtray.

"I sure wish I knew how she does that. I just about peed my pants."

"She doesn't even know how she does it. You're getting better though. I'd say you lasted almost thirty seconds that time." Lydia reached into the bag of cookies and, as she did, slipped a six and a four under it. "I'll see your ten and raise ten."

The other two groaned and dropped in more chips.

"Full house, ladies, aces over queens. Anyone beat that? Didn't think so." Lydia showed her cards and gathered up the chips. "I sure am feeling lucky tonight. Another game?" She ignored the looks she was getting from her sisters and gathered up the cards to play again.

"I'm going to miss this place." Consuelo said as she re-lit her cigar and launched into a coughing fit.

"Consuelo, we've been over this. It's time. Besides, you're going to love Key West, we all are I'm sure." Lydia shuffled the cards.

Josephine started hitting her gagging sister on the back. Lydia took advantage of the distraction to make a few adjustments in the deck as she dealt out the cards.

"Same game, ladies. I guess I'll miss this place a little myself. But you remember, mother said we'd know when to go, and we should just do it when the time came." She finished dealing the cards, and the rest of the deck went on the table.

"Josephine! Take it easy!"

Josephine had gotten into it and was really pounding on her sister's back. As soon as she heard her name, she immediately stopped and picked up her cards. One of her hands disappeared under the table.

Consuelo was wheezing, trying desperately to draw a breath.

Lydia glared at her youngest sister. "Geez Josey, you gotta learn some control! You do that to a normal person, you could hurt somebody!"

Josephine stared at her cards and looked embarrassed. She seemed to be stroking something in her lap.

Lydia was still looking at Josephine while ignoring her other, hyperventilating sister. "And just what do you have under the table?"

Josephine's hand under the table immediately stopped moving. Her eyes looked panicked.

"N-n-n-nothing!"

Lydia still hadn't picked up her cards from the table. She gestured to Josephine.

"Give it to me!"

Josephine frowned, then shrieked, throwing a piece of old fur coat across the table at Lydia. Out of the corner of her eye, Lydia thought she saw movement by her cards just as the moldy fur hit her in the forehead.

She held the fur up between a thumb and forefinger. "Ah gross, Josey! You've got to stop petting things!" She flipped the old piece of fur into a trashcan half filled with Consuelo's beer cans.

Consuelo seemed to have made a sudden recovery from her coughing fit. "I still think she just needs a man to pet."

She looked at her cards and flashed her best sunny smile.

"T-t-two." Josephine looked defiant.

"None for me!" Consuelo was smiling like a finalist for homecoming queen.

Lydia looked at her cards. "Dealer takes three."

She wondered how she had gotten such a lousy hand. She gave Miss Sunshine a look while dealing the cards.

"Like I was saying, Mother said we'd know when it was time to leave here. And we just can't argue with the money Mega Drug coughed up."

For once they were all in complete agreement.

There was a corporate game going on that the sisters had come to know only too well. A game of greed and juvenile one-upmanship that was sweeping the country. Two drugstore chains were building multi-million dollar stand-alone stores in prominent locations everywhere you looked. Each time one company built a new, state-of-the-art store, the other company would quickly build a competing store directly across the street. With interest rates low, drugstores started popping up everywhere. Successful businesses, homes, churches, even hospitals were bought out and bulldozed to make way for the huge modern drugstores.

The health food store across the street from the Majestic Hotel had been demolished just a few months earlier. A shiny new Jack's Drugs now stood in its place.

The financial negotiations with Mega Drug were difficult at first but eventually resulted in the sisters' receiving a very substantial amount for their old hotel, which they used to purchase a small hotel in Key West, Florida.

"You know, maybe we could have held out for more money. Ten to play." Consuelo dropped two five-dollar chips on the table.

"No, the money is more than generous. You just want them to send more muscle to convince the little hotel girls to sell out cheap."

Lydia couldn't help but smile at the memory of the tough guy who came around to scare them into selling out at a ridiculous price. She threw in ten to make sure Consuelo wasn't bluffing.

Both the other young women seemed to be thinking about the big man from Detroit too. They grinned mischievously and squirmed in their seats like little girls.

The first time he came into the hotel, Lydia was at the front desk. He smelled like aftershave and garlic.

"You one of the broads supposed to own this place?"

Lydia smiled across the desk, sizing the guy up. No ring, early forties, big rugged guy, dressed good. Probably a scam,

but not a robbery. She stayed within easy reach of the baseball bat under the desk.

"That would be me!" She gave him a little flutter with
the eyelashes and smiled shyly.

"Well, you get an offer for this old place you might want
to take it. Place like this old hotel could all of a sudden start
having problems, you know? Could get unhealthy here, lose
some value fast. You understand what I'm saying here,
sweetheart?" He looked at his watch.

Lydia did her best to look confused. "I think so. Are you
with the health department?"

She couldn't believe those bastards were pulling this.
Now she knew why they made such a lowball offer for the
hotel.

"No, little lady, I'm not with the health department."
He'd obviously decided she wasn't too bright. "I'm just giving you some friendly advice here. It might be better for
everyone if you just go ahead and sign those papers you got
last week and take the money. That's a lot of money for a
young broad like you. Get smart and take the money so I
don't have to come back."

Lydia took a step back and held a hand to her forehead
like she was about to faint. She was still trembling when the
man looked over his shoulder as he walked out the door.
Lydia ran to the window and checked out his car as he
drove away. She clapped her hands and let out a little squeal
of delight before running off to find her sisters and tell them
the news.

They turned down the drugstore's offer again the next
week, and the man came back. This time they were ready.

As usual, Consuelo was the bait. Her perky, sorority-sis-
ter looks lured the man into the basement after he'd force-

fully mentioned that if they didn't sign the papers he was going to burn the hotel to the ground, with them in it. After the man had been properly secured, they checked his car. Sure enough, the big greaseball had two cans of gasoline in the trunk, along with a nasty-looking sawed-off shotgun.

Three days later the man looked a little dazed as he came out of the basement, but there were no outward signs of what he'd been through. The three sisters solemnly escorted him to the front door. He gave them a long understanding look — a mixture of devotion and blind fear — before he walked back to his car.

Early the next week, the CEO of Mega Drug called. In a shaky voice, he apologized for any misunderstandings and assured them a check would be hand delivered to them for twice the appraised value of the hotel before the end of the week. With the money thing settled, the sisters went looking for a new home.

❧

Josephine slid a ten-dollar chip to the center of the table, then another. She raised an eyebrow in challenge.

"Too rich for me." Lydia dropped her cards and folded.

The other two sisters stared at her for a second, Lydia rarely folded.

Consuelo dropped in a chip. "I'm in. Let's see 'em, Bugs."

Josephine spread out four threes and the Devil.

"Shit." Consuelo threw down her three queens and pair of eights. "And I suppose if you should somehow win tonight you're going to spend your day off with Ben?" Consuelo made some lewd gestures with her hands and contorted her face in mock ecstasy.

Josephine pulled in her winnings and ignored her sister. She smiled and said in a dreamy voice, "Ben."

* * *

Which would be me, Benozzagamii, your typical eight-inch-tall space traveler from Zertron III, the garden planet of the universe. Everyone calls me Ben.

You may wonder how I came to be stranded on a lower-tier planet like earth. I don't blame you, I often wonder myself. All I can say is, if you buy a deeply discounted ticket for a luxury vacation cruise of the universe, be sure to read the fine print. And if you don't read the fine print and find yourself winning really big at star scrabble with the mutant crew of a Kardonian glob freighter, don't drink the green wine.

Anyway, after several months of trying to figure out a way off this primitive rock, I met Josephine. For some reason she was the only human who could see or hear me, so we started hanging out and keeping each other company. Since her sisters couldn't see me, they said I was an "imaginary friend." I certainly wasn't imaginary to Josephine.

It wasn't long before we were more than just friends, and though I am only eight inches tall, we've enjoyed some very intimate times together. This was due in no small part to

Josephine's passionate nature and creative mind. The mango tongue baths helped too.

Anyway, my Josephine was the winner that night at poker, so we spent a thoroughly enjoyable day in the park, lying in the sun, having a great picnic lunch, and catching insects.

A few days later the sisters packed up a big rental truck with all their stuff, and we spent the next five days driving to the other end of the country to start a new life.

Chapter 2

Key West

*The storm clouds came in like schoolyard
bullies. They stole the sun's lunch money and
started throwing raindrops as big as marbles
at everyone on the island.*

A short, chubby, bald man was frantically trying to stuff
two bags of garbage into an already full trashcan outside a
small hotel in Key West. He was getting wet. There was a
can across the street, and he made a run for it. The bags
were throwing off his balance, and the rain made everything
slick. The low stone wall in front of the house that the can
belonged to broke his fall.

He was surprised to find himself unhurt. He was more
surprised to find out he had seriously upset a colony of hon-
eybees who had just recently taken up residence in the wall.

❦

"It's raining again."

Lydia was looking out the window while sitting behind the front desk in the small lobby of their new hotel and home. She'd been going over some paperwork. Josephine had just come in from the garden with some flowers. She put them in a vase on a table.

"They're beautiful, Josey. We've only been here two weeks and you've got that garden looking like something out of a magazine already."

Josephine looked up from arranging the flowers and gave her big sister a smile.

"Th-thanks." She stood back, checked out the flower arrangement, then took out one of the yellow trumpet-shaped flowers and ate it in two bites. Lydia wrinkled her nose.

"Bon appetit."

The rain started coming down hard. Lydia looked out the window again. "I think she goes out to run when it's about to storm just so we'll worry about her."

There was a flash of lightning close by, followed immediately by a huge clap of thunder that shook the windows of the hotel. The front door flew open, and a soaking wet little bald man stumbled in screaming.

"Bees! Killer fucking bees! Get 'em off of me!"

The man collapsed on the floor of the lobby, writhing in pain and swatting at the air. His words became incoherent except for the occasional expletive. The two women stood over the hysterical figure on the floor.

"Geez. It's always something with this guy! I'll get the mop. See if you can find out what's wrong with him, Jos."

While Lydia went off for a mop to clean up the floor, Josephine crouched down for a closer look at the welts on the squirming man's face and hands.

"B-b-bees."

When Josephine got back from her room, the little man was sitting in a different place on the floor. Lydia was mopping up the wet spot. The man was still in a lot of pain and whimpering when the front door flew open and Consuelo stomped in.

"What a rush! I saw lightning hit a tree! There were smoking pigeons everywhere!" She started pulling off the layers of sweatshirts and pants she wore on her daily runs around the island.

Lydia gave her a stern look. "Wet shoes too."

Consuelo saluted her mop-bearing sister and got down to shorts and a T-shirt. She noticed Josephine trying to put salve on the man's bee stings.

"H-hold s-s-st ..."

"What have we here? Somebody got a boo-boo again?" She walked over to have a look.

The little man was wiggling around trying to avoid Josephine's concoction. A glance up and Consuelo was pointing a threatening finger. He became still instantly. The man was wary of the other two, but terrified of the cute little blonde. He had seen what she could do, and he definitely didn't want any of that.

With her patient holding stock still, Josephine finished up quickly, pulled off her rubber gloves, and stood back to admire her work. The man had big purple blotches all over his face, arms, and legs now. The salve burned a little and was starting to itch. The pain was completely gone, but it would be days before the purple stains from the homemade salve wore off.

"B-better?"

Jeremy Donner looked up from the floor at his three employers standing before him and smiled carefully. He wondered how he always seemed to end up working for really sexy, but really scary, women.

"Uh, yeah. Thanks." He looked at the purple blotches on his arms and legs. He thought about his face.

"This stuff does wash off, right?"

After Jeremy had gone to his little room in back and Consuelo had showered, the sisters had a meeting at the front desk.

"Okay, other than the recurring problems with our accident-prone employee, we've got the hotel pretty much under control." Lydia took out a folder from under the desk.

Josephine was leisurely filing her nails. Consuelo was biting hers and looked up from picking her nose.

"I say we can the little worm. We took care of the Majestic by ourselves all right." She produced something from her nose and showed it to Josephine, who handed her a tissue without looking up.

"You know the deal Consuelo, he gets to stay on for at least six months. It was part of the agreement when we bought this place. You can't expect to buy a hotel like this without a few unusual clauses in the contract."

All three sisters smiled at that. It wasn't easy, but they'd found almost exactly what they were looking for — an old two-story hotel in the heart of Key West in good repair.

Almost, in that they would have preferred waterfront, but you could at least see the ocean if you climbed up on the roof. Also, a genuine haunted hotel would have been nice. With the all the ghost stories floating around the island, they were disappointed their new home was without notoriety. Especially when they found out the hotel just down the street had not only a Hemingway room, but an occasional ghost named Robert.

Robert, a mysterious guest, had supposedly blown off the widow's walk during a hurricane seventy years ago and was never found. The story from the local ghost tour had him showing up every few years. The realtor did tell them, though, that Jimmy Buffett was rumored to have stopped in their hotel for a minute once back in the '70s looking for a salt shaker.

But something else had brought the sisters to the island besides the great weather, relaxed atmosphere, interesting people, and the possibility of supernatural phenomena.

"It's time we got serious with our search." Lydia took a computer-printed picture from the folder and set it on the front desk. "We'll make some copies of this to show around. I think Josey did a pretty good job."

Consuelo gave the picture a hard look.

Lydia took the old picture they had seen so many times over the years out of the folder and laid it on the desk. It was the "before" picture, a young woman with a big bleached-blond Mohawk and her eyes closed for the camera. Writing from an ink pen on her eyelids.

"Of course, she might still have the blond Mohawk hair-do and 'EAT SHIT' written on her eyelids. But I kind of doubt it."

Consuelo looked at the second picture, pushed her blond hair up from the sides with her palms, closed her eyes, and asked, "What do you think? Any family resemblance?"

Except for Consuelo with her daily runs, the sisters had been so busy with the hotel that they hadn't been out around town much other than shopping and checking out a couple of bars. There had been a lot to do the first couple of weeks.

Their search was an ongoing thing. In over a year, the only lead had been from a shady LA private eye — a one-way plane ticket had been purchased to Key West within the last few months with the right name.

It was time to hit the streets. Maybe get lucky, at least get a feel for their new town and check out the local color.

* * *

Hey, I think the new place is great! My Josephine is happy to be outside in the garden and there's a big mango tree full of fruit right across the street. The only creepy thing I found so far is the sneaky little guy who works as a handyman at the hotel.

Key West is an expensive place to live, especially for earthlings. Buying the hotel took most of their money, but Josey says she's confident if they work really hard they'll make it as tropical hoteliers. I doubt I could get a job in Key West. Not much work for a small, invisible being with experience as a toll booth operator on a worm-hole bypass. I'd probably have to move to Miami and get a job in politics as a lobbyist.

The hotel is a very old place, but there's modern air-conditioning ductwork running above the ceilings. Not only does that keep the hotel cool, it's a really nice way for someone only eight inches tall to keep an eye on the whole place without having to worry about getting stepped on.

Chapter 3
Local Color

*The sun came up like a big cop walking into
a crowded poolhall on a Saturday night.
Shifty-eyed puddles left from the rain the day
before did their best to look inconspicuous.
They quickly evaporated into the crowd of
humidity milling about the island.*

Orange Dali stood in the shade in front of the Margari-taville Cafe, peeling an orange. He was on his third orange of the morning. There was a place on the concrete next to the bike rack where he had traced a rectangle two feet by three feet with some orange chalk. The thin, dark-haired young man leaned against the tree in front of the bar for a moment looking down, then carefully placed peel inside the border as he took it off the orange.

"Frank, look at this!" A woman tourist wearing a surprised look and a half-bottle of sun block stopped when she saw what the young man next to the tree was doing.

"That's amazing! Look at it, Frank! You got to get a picture of this!" Frank was wearing the look of vacation constipation, and the other half of the bottle of sun-block. He came partially out of his daze and started snapping pictures.

Orange Dali was creating another of his works of art, literally on the streets of Key West. The middle-aged tourist couple's gawking had drawn others from the early shift of wanderers on Duval Street. Inside the chalk frame the young man with the wild eyes and dirty plastic orange cape had placed orange peel, sand, leaves, twigs, gum wrappers, and bottle caps. He'd created a stunning artwork of soft watches hanging from a tree limb. There were even black specks on the faces of the watches for numbers. The specks were dead flies.

"I've never seen anything like that before! It looks ... so real!"

Orange Dali ignored the woman and the others around him. He pulled off the last piece of peel and put the orange in the pocket of his baggy shorts. He absently twisted his long waxed mustache as he walked slowly around his creation. After a moment of close up inspection, he broke the peel into tiny pieces and used them with some sand to create a shadow for one of the watches. The onlookers gasped.

The artist stepped back and regarded his audience for a moment, took off his felt fedora, bowed deeply to the crowd, and dropped the hat to the sidewalk in front of the people. As he posed kneeling beside his latest masterpiece, cameras clicked and money dropped into the hat. When he could see some green sticking up out of the hat, he produced a brush and quickly swept the artwork onto a piece of cardboard and dumped it in a trash can. Several stunned tourists stared at the place on the sidewalk where only a smudged orange chalk frame remained.

Orange Dali walked down Duval Street eating his orange, singing about cheeseburgers in paradise, and telling people, "If you'd like to make a call, please hang up and try again."

The Key West Manor Hotel was only a block over from Duval Street, the main drag in Old Town, and Lydia planned on showing the picture to people working in the shops and bars there. But as she came out the front door of the hotel, she noticed the man who lived in the house across the street was outside. She'd hoped for a chance to meet him, and since he was standing on a stepladder in the front yard, she went for it. As she came through the gate in the low stone wall, she yelled a hello to the man bending over into a tree. She stopped a few feet behind a great-looking butt at eye level.

"Be right with you!"

The man was hammering a piece of tin on the trunk of the tree.

"No hurry!"

Lydia turned her head a little to the side and struck a thoughtful pose. *If the rest is as good as this part of him.*

"There!" He turned around and smiled at her. "Wanted to get that squirrel-guard put on my tree. My mangos have been disappearing lately."

"That so?" *At least as good.* She hadn't gotten a clear look at him from the hotel before. He was gorgeous. Sandy hair, great smile, dressed like he just stepped out of a fashion magazine for tropical casual wear.

"You're the new owner of the hotel, aren't you? Brad's the name." He held out a hand as he stepped off the ladder.

"Lydia. Nice to meet you, Brad." He had the damnedest soft blue eyes she had ever seen. Just give herself a second to look into those eyes. Okay, maybe several seconds.

"So Lydia, if you let go of my hand, we could go inside and I could offer you something to drink."

He was grinning now. Lydia snapped out of it.

"Oh, uh, sorry. Sure." Lydia blushed and followed her new neighbor inside.

It wasn't a big house, but very open and airy. Big windows, ceiling fans, wicker furniture, hardwood floor, bookcase. She checked the books while he went into the kitchen for the drinks. Novels and several cookbooks. He reads and cooks. Lydia put her hand on her chest to steady herself. Brad called out from the kitchen.

"You have someone helping you run the hotel? I've noticed a marked increase in the number of attractive young women over there lately."

"Oh, those are just my sisters, my little sisters. They're actually quite helpless without me." Well, maybe not totally helpless, though she didn't know what they'd do without her to keep them out of trouble. Brad was back.

"Have a seat. It's limeade, made with Key Limes from my tree out back. The squirrels don't seem to be interested in my limes." That smile again.

Lydia sat on the sofa and laid the folder with the pictures in it on the low coffee table. She squirmed a little and looked uncomfortable as she took a sip of her drink.

"Thank you, it's very good."

She squirmed again, and reached behind her and pulled out the hammer he'd been using outside.

"Here, you might need this." She set the hammer on the table in front of her confused host.

"Might need these too." She leaned to one side and pulled out the little jar of nails he'd left on the ladder. She smiled innocently.

"How did you do that?" He stared at his hammer and nails sitting on the table.

"Oh, I learned a few magic tricks from a friend of our mother's." She was enjoying it.

He looked up from the table, giving her his full attention and a wistful smile. "Do you do card tricks, too?"

Lydia snapped her fingers in front of her face, then slowly pulled the Queen of Hearts from her mouth. He watched her hand him the card across the table, then looked at her again.

"That was pretty cool, how ..."

Lydia held her hand up and pointed to the card he was holding. When he looked back at the card it was the King of Hearts. His jaw dropped just a little. Lydia decided to go for the big question.

"You're not gay by any chance, are you?" She bit her lower lip.

Brad regained his composure, "Like a three dollar bill!"

Lydia countered his mischievous grin with a sour frown.

"I don't suppose there's any chance ..."

"I don't think so, Lydia. I'm quite comfortable and happy with my lifestyle choices." He was having much too good of a time with this. "But you didn't come over to discuss my sexual orientation, did you?"

Lydia sighed. She bet he was a great cook too. She reached in the folder.

"No, I wanted to show you this picture. My sisters and I are looking for this person. She may have come to Key West a few months ago."

Brad sipped at his limeaide and looked at the picture.

"My sister Josephine changed the hair and eyes on the computer. The original picture is several years old, and the eyes were closed so she used another picture to get the eyes right. It should be close."

Brad handed the picture back to her. It was a picture of the most average-looking young woman you could imagine.

"Sorry, if I've seen her, I don't remember. Who is she?"

"My sister, my older sister. She ran away from home years ago. We heard she was somewhere in southern California, but we could never find her. Before our mother died just over a year ago, she told us to find her, that we should all be together, even if it was only for a little while." Lydia was surprised she was talking to a stranger like this.

"It was our mother's dying wish that we find our sister Sara."

Consuelo came out the front door of the hotel and saw her big sister going into the house across the street. As smart as her sister was about so many things, Consuelo could never get over how little she seemed to know about men. She shook her head sadly and sighed.

"He's gay Lyd ..."

She might not be as smart as her sister, but Consuelo knew men. Though she'd never met the good-looking guy across the street, she intuitively knew he was gay. It wasn't as useful as some of her sisters' talents, but when you liked men as much as she did, it came in handy.

As she walked through Old Town, her thoughts drifted, as they sometimes did, to what it would be like going away on her own, maybe to the Orient. Plenty of cool martial arts things to get into over there. But she couldn't bring herself to leave her sisters. No telling what would happen to the poor things without her around to protect them.

It was already getting hot, and the late summer humidity was making some of the tourists wandering Duval Street look a little wilted. No sense in bothering with the businesses there; Lydia would be giving the whole area a thorough canvassing in the next few hours.

Consuelo walked down Duval heading for the marina. The place was already getting jammed with walkers and gawkers, bikes and scooters, taxis and trucks, and Conch Train trolleys and Conch Tour buses. Must have been an extra cruise ship or two in port; busy day for the off season.

The heat didn't really bother Consuelo much. She'd already adapted to the new climate. Her body was not only an excellent example of the female form ,\m > it was also tough as a tree stump. She had amazing natural strength and endurance, and added to it with running, martial arts training, weights, and large quantities of food and drink. A large portion of the drink was beer, which she seemed to have an inordinate capacity for.

Her section of town started down by the shrimp boats. She started with a little place trying to look like a local's hangout that offered a free draft beer with every bowl of seafood chowder. She scanned the room stuffed full of eyes and spotted a white-haired old guy sitting at the bar with a parrot on his head. Most of the eyes belonged to tourists, but the old guy looked local. He was barefoot, wearing guano-splattered fisherman's clothes, a captain's hat, and a big smile. Probably a regular at the annual Hemingway Look-Alike Contest.

"Afternoon, young lady! Pull up a stool here and meet Fish Daddy and Capt. Tom!"

The green parrot let loose a loud squawk and a whistle when he heard his name. This was obviously the beginning of a well-practiced bit by the old salt. Consuelo figured he probably got a lot of free beer and female companionship with the routine. For once she wasn't into playing around, she had a lot of territory to cover. Fish Daddy took the picture and gave it a long look before saying anything.

"She in trouble, that why you're looking for her?" The old guy was all business, his act forgotten.

"My sister. I don't really know if she's in trouble or not, but she might have been in Key West a few months ago. Have you seen her?"

The old guy looked at the picture again, set it on the bar and rubbed his face with both hands before answering.

"Might have, but not like you think."

The parrot made a loud belching noise as Consuelo waved off the waitress. Fish Daddy took a long, thoughtful pull on his bottle of beer, then gave her a sideways look.

"I seen somebody look like that in my dreams before, maybe two, three times." He waited a beat, obviously waiting to see how this played. Consuelo held his look. "Your sister a dreamer by any chance? She ever do any lucid dreaming? You know, the kind of dreams when you know you're dreaming, and can control better than regular dreams?"

There was something here. She could tell the old man either had seen someone in his dreams who looked like Sara or at least believed he had.

"I know what lucid dreaming is, but I haven't been in contact with my sister for years, so I don't know if she's a dreamer or not." Lucid dreaming was one of the things her teachers had told her about. As far as she knew though, none of her sisters were serious dreamers. Maybe the old guy was.

"Well, I ain't saying the gal I seen in my dreams was your sister, but whoever she was, she seemed to be in a kinda bad way. Sick, or maybe feeling down, you know?"

"Did you talk to her, in your dreams?"

This wasn't what she had expected to come up with in the search, but she was determined to follow all leads, no matter how strange. Fish Daddy took another meditative slug of beer before answering.

"Not much, a little. Seems like she was looking for someone herself, fella named Charlie if I remember correctly." Consuelo answered his raised eyebrow with a shrug. "Said she was going to ask the Indians about Charlie. I remember that part because she said the Calusa. Ain't been no Calusa Indians for a couple hundred years or so. Made me think maybe she was some kinda lost soul from another time or something."

Consuelo felt a chill run up her spine. She hadn't ever considered her sister Sara might not be with the living anymore.

"Did she say anything else? Anything about where she might be?"

"No, 'fraid not. Must be somewhere in south Florida though; that's where the Calusa used to hang out."

Consuelo killed the glass of beer before she realized she hadn't ordered anything. She gave the old dreamer one of the Hotel's cards and told him to give them a call if he had any more dreams about the woman who looked like Sara. She thanked him for the beer as she slid off the barstool.

"Any time, Missy! If you find your sister, tell her to stop by here sometime. I ain't hard to find!"

Josephine hung out at the front desk of the hotel. Most of the hotel's eighteen rooms were occupied, so somebody had to be at the desk all the time. They hoped to find someone to keep an eye on the place for a few hours once in a while. There was no way they would trust Jeremy to run the place, especially after the reports on his activities from her little Ben. The three sisters wanted to go out together, hit some hot-spots around town, and get out on that beautiful water — plenty of new things to do.

As much as she loved her sisters, Josephine didn't like them calling Ben an imaginary friend, like she was some kind of crazy person. Okay, so maybe she was a tiny bit crazy sometimes, but no doubt they were just jealous of Ben. She'd show them after she found a cure for the common hangover and got filthy rich. Then she'd take a trip with Ben, just the two of them off to some romantic hideaway. Leave her sisters behind. But what would they do without her? Probably be all sickly without someone to take care of them.

Thinking about getting rich, dreaming of romantic getaways with Ben, and worrying about helpless sisters made her hungry, so Josephine whipped up a quick fruit salad of oranges, pineapple, and mango. While eating, she checked out the map of Key West Lydia had worked on the night before. It was marked with the parts of town where each sister would be showing the picture of Sara.

Looked like she had the far end of Old Town, the treasure museum, a few houses, and some restaurants. Josephine wrinkled her nose when she saw how the shaded area on her map went down around the yogurt shop, but included the topless bar. She hated those places. Lydia probably did that on purpose, just to mess with her.

As the day wore on, Josephine checked in an anxious couple from Dayton on their honeymoon and answered the phone. She hated the phone.

By late afternoon she was slumped over the front desk, absently stroking her favorite piece of cashmere. She gazed longingly out the window at the garden of flowering plants and trees, annuals, herbs, birds, and bugs. The side door opened.

"Hey, Josephine! You seen that hammer with the red handle? It's not in the garage."

She rolled her eyes and slowly turned. She regarded the sweaty little purple-spotted handyman with a look of complete boredom.

"S-stone crabs. W-w-wait."

She slipped the old piece of sweater into her pocket and went through the door behind the desk into the kitchen the sisters shared. They had used the hammer the night before for breaking open some crab claws. Stone crabs were the best. She grabbed the hammer and came back up front. Jeremy was looking over the map.

"What's this? You got part of the island marked here for something?"

Josephine stopped a few feet from the desk and narrowed her eyes, holding the hammer menacingly. There was an idea coming. Jeremy lost his usual lecherous glare and took a step back.

"That's the one! You can just give me the hammer now, and I'll be going back to work! Got a lot to do!"

Jeremy was showing a lot of nervous smile. He was supposed to be repairing the wood fence in back, but Ben had
reported seeing him trying to open a trunk one of the guests
had stored in the garage.

Josephine made no move to give up the hammer. Jeremy
was always talking about the topless bar, the Pink Snapper.
He spent a lot of time there, and probably most of his
money. Maybe he could go in there with a picture of Sara to
show around. How bad could he screw that up?

Jeremy looked like he was about to abandon the hammer and flee, so Josephine stopped giving him the eye and
smiled sweetly. She set the hammer on the desk and took
one of the pictures of Sara out and laid it next to the hammer.

"L-look at th-this."

Jeremy cautiously approached the far end of the desk.
He picked up the picture and gave it a good look.

"T-take that to the S-snapper. A-a-ask if..."

"Hey, this looks kinda like Sara!"

Gustov flipped a cigarette butt out the car window at
some freak with a plastic orange cape.

"Definitely got your more loony types well represented
in this town. Check the one in the cape with the mustache
having a conversation with himself. Whole town's supposed
to be spaz cases and fags. Least that's what the boss says."
He looked over at the smaller man sitting next to him in the
driver's seat.

Louie usually didn't mind his partner's bullshit, but it
was getting on his nerves today. The rental car's air-conditioning had crapped-out halfway down from Miami. He was

sweating like a pig already, and getting stuck behind some big smelly delivery truck on Duval Street wasn't helping the heat rash he could feel cooking down between his legs. He wasn't having one of his better days. He needed a shower, maybe two.

"There aren't any more weirdos here than Miami, Gus. They just put up with 'em here, think they're cute or something. People come from all over the country to get sunburned and look at the freaks. They get 'em all over at a place called Mallory Square every day and let 'em act-up. Tourists come look at the sunset, give the freaks money. Real unsanitary situation."

Louie brushed some imaginary dust off his white linen jacket and blew the car horn at the truck. While Gustov went for the fat and sloppy look, Louie favored the Miami Vice style. He had Don Johnson's wardrobe, right down to the Italian shoes and no socks. The fact that Johnson was a cop in the old TV series and he was a small-time hood didn't make much difference to Louie.

He'd been to Key West before; Gustov hadn't. Louie had been all over the country; Gustov hadn't been out of Miami in years. Louie had pulled a lot of scams, done some debt collections, worked a few people over pretty good even, but never done any real wet work. Gustov had. So you had to give the man a certain amount of respect, even if he did have some rather unsanitary habits himself.

Consuelo went to the marina office and showed some people the picture. Nothing. A guy fishing off the dock said he might have seen someone who looked like that, but he couldn't be sure. She worked some of the bigger boats and houseboats that looked like they'd been there for a while. No luck. Time for a break.

There was a good-looking young guy scrubbing down a small sailboat. Gave her a look and a smile. Said he was sailing around by himself before starting law school. Nice guy. She could tell. Consuelo's sharp blue eyes softened, they took on more the look of a big cat. He offered her some Gatorade and she drank a quart without looking away. Sometimes, like now, she purred.

A half hour later she was using the shower in the little head of the sailboat. After getting back in her clothes she gave him a quick kiss and left him smiling in his bunk to work on the story he was no doubt going to tell his friends back at school about the blond in Key West.

Several of the bigger private boats were empty, but there was a guy sitting in the shade on an old houseboat at the end of the dock. The houseboat looked like someone had put a lot of work into it.

"Hi. I've got a picture here of someone I'm looking for. Mind if I come aboard so you can take a look?"

The man had been looking down, holding something in his hand. He looked up and tilted his hat back a little. "Sure, come on aboard young lady. Have a seat, take a load off. Get out of that hot sun for a bit."

The guy was a weathered-looking old dude sporting a big goofy grin. Consuelo had a seat at his little table. There was some fishing tackle on the table, mostly hooks and line. He picked up a piece of heavy line about a foot long and handed it to her.

"I don't suppose you could give me a hand here for just a sec could you? I got a little problem here, and another pair of hands would be a help."

He opened his hand and there was a small gold hook stuck deep in the palm of his hand.

"I was just tying some bait hooks here and got myself hooked good swatting at a deerfly."

He had Consuelo loop the line through the bend in the hook, and while he was pushing down on the shank, he told her to give it a quick yank. She was skeptical, but it popped out clean.

"Cool! Hey, can I try that?"

Before the old guy could say anything, Consuelo had picked up one of the small hooks on the table and jammed it in her hand up past the barb. He stared, dumbfounded, at the scarred and calloused hand with the hook sticking out of it.

"Don't that hurt a bit, Miss? I seen a lot of people get hooked, myself more often than I like to think about, but I never seen anyone do it on purpose."

Consuelo shrugged and held out her hand. While she pushed down on the hook, the man put one end of the line through and gave it just a little pressure.

"Okay, here we go, miss, on three. One, two ...," and he popped the hook out.

"Hey that's some trick, mister!" Consuelo licked the little drop of blood off her hand and stuck out the other for a handshake.

"Consuelo!"

"Name's Hank, but most folks call me Slip. Glad to make your acquaintance there, young lady."

He tried not to show it, but Consuelo saw the surprised look in his eyes from the handshake. She took out one of the pictures.

"This is a picture of my sister. We think she came to Key West a few months ago."

The old guy was giving the picture a good look.

"Cool old houseboat you got here."

The man looked up with the grin again. "That it is, but it's not mine. Belongs to a fella name a Taco Bob. He's off somewhere fishing. Man's all the time off fishing." He handed the picture back. "I'm sorry, Consuelo, but I ain't seen her, least if I did I don't remember. You might want to ask Taco Bob sometime. Man knows a lot a folks around here, and known to help 'em out whenever he can."

"Maybe I could leave one of these pictures with you, and you could show it to him?"

The old guy looked like he could take care of himself. Tough-looking customer if you looked past the goofy grins. She wasn't sure what to make of this guy. Not an easy read, even for her.

"Hey, no problem, young lady. Be glad to help out."

Consuelo left him a picture with the hotel's phone number. She could tell he was watching her as she walked back up the dock.

Jeremy's life had had its ups and downs in his almost forty years. Not long ago he'd been broke with no job and no friends. Then fate sent him a fellow connoisseur of au naturel women at the topless bar — a regular who owned a hotel. The man liked Jeremy, especially when he was loaded, which he usually was, but lived in fear of his lovely but totally cold-hearted-bitch wife.

Jeremy talked his way into a job at the hotel. The handyman job came with a salary and a little room in back. Things were looking up.

The wife's poodle soon changed everything by running out in the street in front of a speeding beer truck one night. The wife nearly made a daring rescue.

After the funeral, the widower found a buyer for the hotel. He was feeling the glow of champagne and being newly engaged to one of the dancers at the topless club when he decided to put in the contract that the handyman had six months to find suitable employment elsewhere.

The new owners of the hotel were three very fine-looking sisters from out West.

Shortly after Jeremy thought he recognized a picture the youngest and hottest of the sisters had shown him, he woke up in her bedroom. The curtains were drawn and the room was lit with candles. The air was thick with strange incense. As he came fully awake, Jeremy noticed the decor of the room was like something out of an old Bella Lugosi movie, one of the really creepy ones. It was complete with a big four-poster bed, long dark curtains, some dusty cobwebs, and what appeared to be a fully stocked alchemist's laboratory.

He first realized something wasn't right when he couldn't move his head. He seemed to be sitting in a high-back chair, with several hundred feet of telephone cable wrapped around him and the chair. The only things he could move were his eyes, fingers and toes. Looking down, the chair seemed to be sitting in a large metal wash tub. He tried to yell, but there were enough wraps of cable in his mouth that he couldn't get out much more than a moan.

"Look who's awake!"

The little blonde, Consuelo, came into the room. He had seen her kick the living shit out of a big obnoxious drunk outside the hotel one night. She was currently drinking out of a quart bottle of beer and giving him the same kind of cold smile he had seen on bar-bouncers just before they threw someone, often himself, out the front door.

"Josey! You're patient is awake!" Consuelo was up for a closer look.

He realized something was hanging out of his nose. Josephine came in the room and clapped her hands, then rubbed them together in anticipation.

"Gotta hand it to you Jos, this is a great idea. All that hair coming out of his nose always did look pretty gross."

Consuelo leaned in closer and wrinkled her nose. She lightly touched whatever it was hanging out of his left nostril. Jeremy tried to tell them fun was fun, and he was ready to be untied and go to his room. It just sounded like a lot of moaning though, with all the cable in his mouth.

"Don't spill the beans yet, Jeremy! Josey hasn't even started! Anyway, you had your chance already when she asked how you knew the woman in the picture was named Sara. She says you got all secretive and wouldn't tell, remember?"

Jeremy did remember, come to think of it. He was thinking that maybe he should have been a little more forthcoming with what he knew. Consuelo stepped to the side, and Josephine was standing in front of him with a cordless drill in her hands. He was real sure he should have been more forthcoming.

Lydia tried numerous places on Duval, showing the picture to a lot of people with no luck. A few maybes, but that was about it. Did get to see the inside of some interesting places, and talked to some unique, and sometimes quite odd, people. Key West definitely was different from Pine Cove.

It was going to take a few more days just to get Old Town covered. She hoped Consuelo had gotten lucky. Actually she probably had, knowing her appetite and intuitive powers when it came to men. Maybe she had gotten lucky in finding out something about their missing sister too.

Brad had told her to stop by anytime, so she made up an excuse to pop in for a minute on her way back to the hotel.

Walking across the street from Brad's to the hotel, Lydia was still thinking about the recipe for baked triggerfish he'd told her about. When she came in the front door of the hotel, there was a terrible crash. She ran to the back.

"What's all this?"

∽

They were setting Jeremy and his chair back up in Josephine's room when Lydia came in. Josephine's idea for nose hair removal had worked even better than they had hoped. Their first client had become a little over-excited when the drill had been attached to the drill bit glued to his nose hairs however. When the drill was switched on, he had somehow jumped enough to topple his chair and the metal tub it was sitting in.

"Josey has found a new way to get rid of unsightly nose hair!"

Consuelo was giving her big sister her best sunny smile, which Lydia completely ignored as she walked over for a closer look at Jeremy's nose.

"Nice job, all right."

She looked at the one clean nostril and panicked eyes of their bound, gagged, and moaning employee.

"Although I somehow suspect he didn't volunteer for this important breakthrough in male grooming." Lydia gave her sisters a disapproving look.

Josephine had taken the furry drill bit out of the drill and was putting some glue on another one. She gestured toward the phone cable wraps, "F-for his own p-p-pro-tec-tion."

Consuelo stood behind the chair and held Jeremy's head while her sister stuck the gluey drill bit in the other nostril. Lydia looked again at her sisters, and from the dead serious stares she got back, she knew it was something important. Consuelo filled her in.

"He saw one of the pictures Josey had and knew her name was Sara. Then decided he didn't want to talk about it."

Jeremy stopped moaning and looked at Lydia with pleading eyes. She looked at Josephine.

"Give me the drill, Josey."

*   *   *

The superglue and drill idea was mine actually. Guy really did have a bad nose hair problem. I got a good seat up above in the air vent and watched the fun. After Lydia took a turn with the drill, Jeremy told all he knew about Sara.

I'm thinking he might be hearing me lately. In the morning, while I was making my rounds through the hotel air conditioning system, I stepped in a mousetrap someone had set inside the vent to Jeremy's room. I've still got a bump

on my head from it. That's when I first got the
idea for the speedy nose-hair removal system.
Later, I'm going down into Jeremy's room.
Maybe dig a little hole in his bed pillow and
take a crap in it.

Chapter 4
Plans

A breeze blew into town after dark. The startled palm fronds rattled, the boats in the marina rocked, and an early-evening drunk on Duval Street went stumbling after his hat. The breeze looked around, decided it didn't like what it saw, and left. The breeze could come and go as it pleased.

Two figures sat at the end of a scarred old mahogany bar in a dimly lit place with no name on the rough side of town. It was early evening, and there wasn't much of anyone else in there yet. A big guy with something-or-other Biological on his sweatshirt sat with a middle-aged hippie at a table along the wall. They were drinking bottled beer and having a heated philosophical discussion.

The front door opened and a low-tide-scented gust of wind blew into the barroom. The two figures turned on their stools just enough to check out a tall, heavy-set man in slacks and a short-sleeve shirt walking in the bar with a small man in a tropical suit.

The newcomers ordered drinks and took them to a table in back. They sipped their drinks and looked bored. Out of habit, they kept an eye on the few other patrons in the oldest and least known bar in Key West.

"I can't believe you wanted to come in here, Louie. This place is a fucking dump."

Louie was feeling better after a long shower, a generous handful of talcum powder on his crotch, and the first hit off his drink.

"True, it's not one of your more hygienic places on the planet, but I always feel relaxed here. Supposed to be where old Hemingway went when he got thrown out of the other bars. Drinks are cheap, best view in Key West, and nobody fucks with you."

For the kind of money he was being paid for the job, Louie shouldn't mind being in the dark about just what the job entailed. But he did mind. Joey Two Thumbs told him back in Miami to take orders from this big goon Gustov, and he'd be filled in once they got to the Keys. Gustov seemed to be half-listening to the big guy and the hippie bitching about how some marina up around Sanibel was going to hell lately.

"So Gus, my man, you ready to fill me in on this job we got going here?"

Louie sipped his drink through the little straw you were supposed to use for stirring your drink. Gustov hated it when people did that, which is exactly why Louie did it.

"Job might be big. Depends." He leaned in closer and lowered his voice. "Might just be some surveillance, or maybe we lean on some people a little. We get the right weather, might be big. Real big." Gustov leaned back in his chair and gave his junior partner a smirk to let him know that was all he was getting for now.

"Big? How big? We going to wet someone here or what? There's ..."

Gustov held up his hand to signify the discussion was over.

"Hey, it's not like I don't have a right to know ..."

Louie was pissed, but decided to let it go when he realized his partner was enjoying holding back. They looked out the big windows at the winking lights of a small marina, past the two rumpled-looking figures talking quietly at the end of the bar.

"Check it out, Gus. I think one of those things at the bar might be a woman. Good-looking guy like you ... ."

Gustov turned and glared at his grinning partner who started making slurping sounds by sucking up the last of his drink with his stir stick.

Neither of the people at the end of the bar were very big. The one who seemed to have one shoulder higher than the other coughed and spit on the floor. She ran her fingers through her ratty brown wig.

"So we know she was h-here, she was d-definitely in Key West."

Josephine had been in the bar once before, and her stuttering hadn't been bad then either. The old bar relaxed her.

Lydia was dressed as a man, old fisherman's clothes, hair tucked up in a hat, and some grime on her face. Josephine was wearing baggy clothes and doing her gimp routine. Got them in the bar without a second look. The make-up thing Consuelo did on her sisters made sure no one would bother them. Facial sores and warts were her specialty. Halloween had always been much more fun than Christmas.

"We've got a pretty good idea what she's been up to the last few years now, but we still don't know where she is."

Lydia motioned to the bartender who brought them fresh drinks and looked at the picture that was handed over. The bartender looked even rougher than either of the two sisters, and there wasn't any make-up involved. Tattoos, piercings, scars, shaved head, big shoulders, permanent scowl, and a limp. Couldn't tell if it was a man or woman either. Lydia was leaning more toward man; Josephine was still undecided. She took a sip of her club soda with Key Lime. Lydia was drinking draft beer. After a good look, the bartender shook his/her head, handed the picture back, and went down to the other end of the bar.

"S-she's not in southern California. N-not from what J-Jeremy said about her t-taking those things from that cult out t-there."

The wind was really whipping in the darkness outside. They looked out the windows overlooking some sailboats rocking in the marina. Josephine started carving her name in the bar with a razor-sharp steel fingernail she had glued onto her finger.

The door opened and a well-dressed old man came slowly in with a young blonde on his arm. They sat at a table by the window. The woman came to the bar to get drinks while the old man carefully took something out of his pocket. He placed what looked like a tiny stuffed dog on the table.

"No, I doubt she went back there." Lydia was looking over her sister's shoulder at what turned out to be a real dog, a really old Chihuahua wearing sunglasses. "He said the last time he saw her, she was walking toward the marina area. Maybe we should try there again."

A deeply tanned man with shifty eyes came in the bar with a young woman sporting buzzcut hair and a black man in a highway patrol uniform. They sat at the other end of the bar. The woman had fishing flies for earrings, complete with hooks.

"I d-don't trust Jeremy. I t-think there's something he's not t-telling us."

Lydia knowingly avoided the fierce look in her sister's eyes. Those weren't the eyes of a stage mesmerist; little Josey's eyes were the real thing.

"Now, Josephine. I think we got all the pertinent information from the little weasel we need."

Josephine added a frown to her fierce look.

"We'll keep asking around with the picture for a few more days. If we don't find out anything, you can have him for more of your experiments. Okay?"

Josephine raised an eyebrow and seemed to be in deep thought for a few seconds before making up her mind.

"D-deal!" She smiled for her sister, showing plenty of yellow and black teeth, another of Consuelo's touches.

"God, but you're a pretty little thing tonight, Josey." Lydia gave a sick look and stuck her tongue out a little.

A big cockroach ran across the top of the bar and Josephine stabbed it with her steel fingernail. She held up her squirming trophy, popped her mouth open, and very slowly started moving the roach in.

"Please don't do that Josey, not here."

Lydia looked over at the two men who had just come in. The tall thin man with wild eyes and flecks of gray in his hair took a seat at the bar, while his overweight and inebriated friend headed for the can. As he staggered past the sisters, Josephine flicked the roach onto the back of the man's neck. It ran down inside his collar just as he went into the men's room. The other man smiled and nodded his head approvingly at the good shot. Josephine showed the man some teeth and picked at her face. The man quickly looked away and attempted to engage the bartender in a discussion of the historical aspects of the bar.

Josephine regarded her sister carefully. "Y-you're looking p-pretty hot tonight t-too sis." A big lewd wink. "You t-think Brad across the s-s-street would go for some of th-that?"

Both sisters smiling big.

"I may just have to try it sometime, little sister." Lydia fluttered her eyelashes provocatively and gave a big sigh.

A tall man wearing a skirt or a kilt and a plastic shower cap came in and sat at the bar next to Lydia. He had something wrapped in bloody newspaper tucked under his arm. The man glanced over and gave her a nod before ordering himself a drink. He tossed the drink down and headed back out the door. The sisters looked at the bartender who shrugged his/her shoulders.

Lydia stood, stretched, and gave her crotch a quick pull. The sisters killed their drinks in unison and slammed their glasses on the bar.

Lydia tried to make her voice deeper, "Come on, honeypie, let's get out of here. Place is getting too many weirdos in it!"

The whole bar watched as Lydia walked out the door with a hunchbacked Josephine hobbling along behind, snarling and spitting as she went.

∞

One reason hardly anyone knew about the oldest bar in Key West is because it isn't in Key West. The bar with no name is actually on Stock Island, the next island up the Keys.

The Key West Manor Hotel, itself in the middle of the island of Key West, had come with not only a horn-dog handyman, but with a car as well. The sisters' ride back to the hotel from the bar was a mid-'80s Cadillac convertible beater with a very custom paint job. There was a hand-painted sunrise on the hood and a sunset on the trunk. The years of salt air were beginning to take their toll on the old car, despite being kept in the garage at the hotel, Consuelo had already taken it to a shop and had it tuned up. It looked a little rough but ran out just fine.

As they pulled onto A1A, a figure ran out of the bushes and grabbed something from along the side of the road, then disappeared into the darkness.

"Was that him? The guy from the bar?"

"L-l-looked like him!"

"I guess we know now what he had in the newspaper." Lydia felt her stomach do a little jump.

The wind had calmed, and the lights from the land reflected off the flat, black water in the distance. With the top down on the car, it was a nice night for a drive. They drove up the keys for a while just enjoying the night air before turning around in the parking lot of a big new restaurant called Governor's Chicken Burritos. A sign out front said opening soon.

"Hey, that sounds good. Have to give it a try sometime."

Josephine stuck out her tongue, then put a finger in her open mouth. Lydia shrugged.

"You know, one reason we never heard from her for so many years is probably because those cults aren't real big on their members contacting family."

"B-brainwashed?"

"Maybe. Though I kind of doubt it if she grabbed some of their stuff and beat it on her own from California down here. I wonder what she was up to?"

"M-m-maybe she went b-b-back to Pine C-Cove, looking for us."

"If she does, she's bound to ask around when she finds the Majestic is gone. We did leave her picture and our new address with the flower shop next door."

They drove on in silence for a few minutes.

"She p-probably doesn't know a-about m-mom."

Lydia could see the tears shining in her sister's eyes in the darkness. "No, she probably doesn't. We'll have to deal with that when we find her."

She reached over and gave Josephine's hand a little squeeze. She wanted to change the subject. It was too nice of an evening, riding in the open-air car, to dwell on unhappy things. True to her overly emotional personality, Josephine had taken their mother's death the hardest. Lydia knew if she let her, Josephine would be upset the rest of the evening.

"So Josey, how's your new medicine coming? Any progress to report on finding the cure for the common hangover?" Lydia hoped the mention of her sister's favorite project would take her mind off their mother's passing.

"T-t-trying a n-n-new po-potion. T-t-t-t..." Josephine became frustrated with her stuttering and hit the dashboard of the car with her fist. "S-s-s-sh-shit!"

They crossed a small bridge and were in Key West proper. There was enough light from the streetlights for Lydia to see what Josephine was signing. Her hands were flying. She could sign like nobody's business.

"Consuelo's not such a good test subject though. True, she does drink enough to have some pretty serious hangovers, but she's such a tough little shit, the booze doesn't seem to have much effect on her."

Lydia was trying to watch her sister's quick hands and the road. A taxi blew its horn at the weaving Caddy, both women immediately gave it the finger.

"Well, there shouldn't be any shortage of hangovers in this town to try it out on. If you're going to try it out on Jeremy, try not to kill the little perv, at least not until he finishes fixing the roof."

Josephine pantomimed someone drinking and then taking a long fall. Their laughter carried over the calm black water.

*   *   *

I've been helping Josephine with her hangover medicine. I think we're getting close, too. One thing we have to work out is the little problem with Jeremy's body wanting to violently reject anything resembling food for 24 hours after taking the cure.

Jeremy must not have liked what I did to his pillow. The next day I was watching him hard at work in his room trying to alter some lottery tickets, and he kept stealing little glances up toward the air vent. I came back by later and the air duct smelled like someone had sprayed bug-killer up there. I figured two could play that game. While he was off at the topless bar I drug a smelly fish head from the garbage and put it in the vent. Then I took some screws out of the stepladder.

Chapter 5
Dinner

*The thunderstorm had just come into
existence, and already it was in a mood.
Dizzy from too much early afternoon
humidity and cheap sunshine, it came
barreling down the backroads of the
turquoise sea. It swerved to get a sailboat
headed for the reef and completely missed the
island.*

Jeremy had been watching for a storm and was pissed
that one just missed the island. Now he had to go up on the
roof of the porch overlooking the pool. There was a hole
where a tree branch had fallen. He'd managed to put off the
job for several days, but it looked like he had run out of
excuses and was going to have to do some actual work.

"Looks like that storm missed us, Jeremy. Better get up
there and patch that roof." Lydia was cleaning leaves out of

the pool with a long-handled net. "And don't tell me you need something else from the hardware."

Jeremy dejectedly looked at the roofing materials and tools on the ground next to the ladder. He had spent several days collecting everything he'd need, right down to the proper color shingles. The sisters had been placing bets on how long it would take him to fall off the roof. Luckily, the hole was in the porch roof, which wasn't that high and above some shrubs. Just a few days earlier he'd fallen off a stepladder in his room.

"I don't know, Lydia, those thunderstorms are tricky sometimes. Big storm like that could turn around and come back here real fast."

They both looked in the direction the storm had gone. Lydia shook her head and pointed at the ladder. Jeremy sighed and did his best to swallow his fear of heights as he picked up his tools and climbed the ladder. Lydia clicked the stopwatch hanging around her neck and went inside.

Maria, the woman who cleaned rooms at the hotel, had gone for the day and Consuelo was running the front. She took care of guests and in between worked out behind the desk. She had weights and would do staggering numbers of sit-ups and push-ups.

A couple from Minnesota had just checked out. They loved the hotel, the beautiful weather, even the gaudy tourist shops of Duval Street, but they mostly talked about the funny artist with the plastic orange poncho he wore like a cape. Or at least the woman talked about it, the man just looked uncomfortable.

"It was the damnedest thing you ever seen, honey! He just took all this stuff, little pieces of trash it was, and made this beautiful Dali artwork! The guy must be a little off if you ask me, because he just swept it all up when he got done and threw it in the garbage can! Luckily we got some pictures to show when we get back home. You mind if I take one of these?"

The woman pointed to a bowl of fancy hotel match-books next to a bowl of mints.When Consuelo smiled and nodded, the woman took a fistful out of the bowl and stuffed them in her purse. Then as Consuelo turned around to put the room key on the board, the woman grabbed another big fistful. The husband looked away. He was used to it.

"We're having the early-bird dinner at that big restaurant next to the marina. I want to get a good meal because they hardly give you anything on the plane anymore. Isn't that right, Frank?"

Frank was staring out the window at the young woman working in the garden. It was hard not to stare. She was very attractive, and wearing only a bikini top and shorts. She moved her hand quickly in the mulch, and came up with something. She popped it in her mouth, then looked toward the window and smiled just as he heard his name.

"Frank, are you listening to me?"

Frank was startled.

"That young woman! I think she just ate ..."

His wife pushed him aside for a look.

"Quit looking at her, you're old enough to be her father! I don't know why you always have to embarrass me like this!"

Consuelo took a peek out the window at her sister pulling weeds. The woman slipped a big handful of mints into her purse and headed for the door, Frank in tow with their hotel-towel-stuffed luggage.

"We've got to run if we're going to get to the restaurant in time for the special. Thanks for everything, sweetie!"

The days since the sisters learned Jeremy had seen Sara in Key West had been busy. They were still showing the picture around town but weren't getting any more positive hits. All they had to go on was what Jeremy had told them. That and the crazy old guy who'd told Consuelo he saw Sara in his dreams.

The big news otherwise had been a letter — a letter from MegaDrug offering to buy the hotel. The sisters were finding it hard to believe and thought it was a prank. No way that could be happening to them again. There must be some mistake. Lydia called the number in the letter, and it was for real: MegaDrug offered a deal to buy them out lock, stock, and barrel.

The sisters talked it over that night over cards. They decided MegaDrug must send out a bunch of letters every time they were going to move into another area.

Of course they didn't have any intention of selling this time, not at any price. They felt at home in Key West, and the hotel was just what they had been looking for. It was a bit troubling though that the offer was considerably less than what they had paid just a few weeks earlier. They agreed it might be a good idea to keep an eye out for trouble, just in case.

❧

Josephine came in with the mail a few minutes after the Minnesotans had hurried off to their discount dinner.

"We get any more offers from drug companies, Josey?"

Consuelo was doing squats behind the desk, and only her head and shoulders showed as she came up each time. Josephine looked through the mail as she walked across the lobby.

"Nope. B-b-bills."

There was a pounding noise from the back of the hotel. Both women stopped what they were doing and looked in the direction of the noise.

"T-t-twenty minutes. Y-you?"

Consuelo resumed her squats.

"I'm down for a half-hour, and I'm feeling lucky."

Consuelo gave her sister a big wink the next time up. There was a loud crash, and both women ran for the back of the hotel, then realized the noise came from the kitchen. They looked in and found Lydia picking up the pieces from a box of old dishes that had fallen from the table.

"N-need help?"

Lydia was pretty embarrassed, she usually didn't break things.

"Yeah, as a matter of fact, I could use some help getting things ready. Brad's coming over for dinner this evening. I guess I'm a little nervous."

Consuelo couldn't help herself.

"He's gay, you know."

Lydia was holding a particularly nasty-looking shard of porcelain in a menacing way. She gave her sister a hard look.

"Yes, sister mine, so you've mentioned. Several times."

Consuelo gave a nervous laugh before quietly slipping back to the front desk. Josephine started sweeping broken dishes into a cardboard box.

"Don't m-mind her." Lydia broke her stare from where Consuelo had left the room and went back to putting the bigger pieces in the trashcan.

"She's right, though. I keep thinking we can just be friends and all that crap, but I got it bad for this guy." Lydia sighed.

Josephine, who was in love with an eight-inch-tall alien who might not even exist, came over and gave her big sister an understanding hug.

Jeremy didn't actually fall off the roof. He was pulling back the old shingles around the hole and slipped, then slid down the sloping roof on his belly for twenty feet. When he stopped, his legs dangled over the edge. His screams brought the three sisters and two guests out to investigate.

After assuring the guests everything was all right, that he did this sort of thing all the time, a decision had to be made. Did his current position count as a fall, or not. Jeremy's shirt had ridden up his belly on the slide down, and the road rash from the rough shingles really stung.

"Come on here! I can't hold on much longer! Somebody give me a hand!"

On cue, the three sisters broke into a rousing golf clap, then went back to their debate.

"It's not a fall until he hits the ground!" Lydia checked the stopwatch. "Anyway, it's a moot point because in a few minutes ..."

Consuelo pointed and asked what kind of parrot that was way over there, then jumped up and grabbed a foot. Jeremy lost his precarious hold and screamed a really good one before hitting the ground.

"N-n-now look! You k-killed him!"

Lydia clicked the stopwatch and checked Jeremy. "Nah, he's faking it. Though wetting his pants was a good touch."

Jeremy opened his eyes a little to check his pants.

"Ha! Caught you looking." Consuelo grabbed him under the arms and pulled him to his feet. "A little scratched up, but he looks all right to me."

Josephine put on some disposable gloves and gave him a quick check for anything broken. The dazed little man held still, hoping for something broken so he wouldn't have to go back up.

"I think my ankle's broken, or maybe my leg. Maybe both."

Josephine gave his leg a check and pronounced him unbroken. Consuelo smiled.

"You couldn't have broken your leg anyway, you landed on your belly. Plenty of padding there." She pulled up Jeremy's shirt and gave him a slap on his scratched and pro-truding belly that sounded a lot worse than it was.

"Ouch! Shit that hurts! I think I might have internal injuries here!"

Consuelo took a step back and snapped a sidekick a quarter inch from Jeremy's nose that made him forget about his belly.

"Back to work, Jeremy, or you'll have an internal injury from my foot up your ass."

Jeremy gave the sisters his best hurt-puppy look and started back up the ladder. If he got done before dark, he wouldn't have to go back up again the next day. Being a roofer in the blazing sun of Key West was no joke.

Consuelo was all smiles.

"So, looks like I win!"

The sisters watched Jeremy until he was on the roof, then started back inside. Lydia put her arm around Consuelo's shoulders and clicked her stopwatch.

"Double or nothing?"

❧

Tuna kabobs were her first choice, but the fish market was out of tuna. Lydia decided to go with broiled pompano with conch salad, baked new potatoes, marinated cucumbers, steamed green beans, and homemade Key Lime Pie. She was determined to show off her cooking skills for Brad.

'This looks really great, Lydia! Did you do all this yourself?"

Other than a couple of Jeremy breaks, Lydia had been working like a cart donkey for hours preparing the meal. She smiled a shy smile at Brad.

"Oh, it's just a little something I whipped up."

Consuelo didn't hesitate and started helping herself to the food. "Yeah, good-looking eats, Sis!" She loaded her plate and attacked.

"You'll have to excuse Consuelo, Brad; she's a growing girl."

Lydia gave her sister a warning look. Consuelo glanced across the table from Brad and gave their guest a big wink.

"Well, I haven't had pompano in a while. It's actually one of my favorites." Brad helped himself to a serving of everything and dug in.

"There's pie too. The limes you gave me yesterday from your tree." Lydia was proud of that.

"Oh really? I'm impressed Lydia." They were both smiling big.

Josephine was picking at her salad. She didn't eat much, not at the table at least. She took the smallest piece of fish on the platter for herself and tried a little bite. Brad was noticing. Lydia noticed Brad noticing.

"And Josey here is a picky eater. She just eats mostly salad, fruit, and some fish. Very delicate little flower she is." Josephine fluttered her eyelashes at Brad and gave him a coy look. "She likes to eat things right out of the garden too, but we won't go into that."

Consuelo came up for air after a big pull on her beer mug. "Yeah, she likes to eat bugs, mostly."

Consuelo's eyes got big for a second, and then tears came to her eyes. Lydia had taken off her shoe and had a death grip on her sister's Achilles' tendon with her toes. It was her one weak spot.

Brad was smiling, but wary.

"Is that so, Josephine? You eat bugs?"

Josephine looked him square in the eye with her most serious look.

"Yes!"

She surprised herself as much as her sisters by not stuttering. She held her head high and smiled as though she had just delivered a major speech.

"Brad, Josey's a little, different." Lydia had been going over all day how she was going to explain her sisters. "She studied a lot of diet books and is into her own version of the Paleolithic Diet. It's pretty much what monkeys eat: certain leaves, fruit, some meat, and yes, bugs. It doesn't seem to be hurting her any, and she looks healthy enough."

Josephine stood and stuck her ample chest out and strutted once around the table like a fashionably bored model on a runway. Consuelo provided commentary, using a loaf of French bread for a microphone.

"And next is Princess Bug Breath, that slinky temptress of the tropics, with a form fitting Sloppy Joe's wife-beater top and shocking-pink shorts with a dirt smudge on the bottom that say, 'I'm hot!'"

Josephine stopped when she got back to her chair, turned around and shook her ass at everyone, then sat back down and resumed picking at her food.

Brad was having a good time. He gave Josephine a round of applause and went back to his pompano.

"Josey can't talk real good, usually. Stutters, you know." Consuelo was chewing a big mouthful of bread. "She's a little crazy too."

That got her some looks, so she quickly added, "But then our teachers said we were all a little off."

She came up with a weak smile and got interested in her food again.

Brad wasn't going to argue the point. "I bet you ladies were a real challenge for your teachers in school all right." Everyone looked at Lydia.

"We mostly behaved in school. We made a point not to stand out or draw too much attention to ourselves. The teachers my sister is referring to are the special teachers we had."

A fly made a quick treetop pass over the dinner table. The two younger sisters noticed. Lydia continued.

"We lived with our mother, but we spent time with a couple of her friends who taught us things they didn't teach

in school. One of them was a man who was a guest sometimes at our hotel named Logan. He was off on his travels to
the Orient a lot, but always spent time with us when he was
around. He had some really fantastic stories of his travels
and the strange people he knew over there. Great stuff for
girls who hardly ever went anywhere. He was quite the master in martial arts and taught Consuelo a lot of survival stuff
too."

Consuelo narrowed her eyes and tried to look shifty. The
fly made another low pass over the table, then circled back
for some altitude and a better look at all the food in the tar-
get area. Brad noticed the fly, and that Consuelo and
Josephine were both locked onto it but weren't letting on.
Lydia continued.

"He used to take her up in the mountains in the win-
ter and leave her up there with no clothes or anything.
She learned how to make a knife out of rock and how to
make a fire with just sticks. Left her up there for five days
once during Christmas break. She came back wearing
some clothes made out of vines and animal fur. Had to get
her own food too. Gained two pounds as I remember."
Consuelo held up three fingers and continued eating without looking up. Lydia nodded. "I stand corrected, Ninja-
Girl.

"Logan taught us first-aid at an early age. When Consuelo started to climb trees in dangerous ways and devel-
oped a knack for falling and breaking things, we practiced
on her. By the time she was ten, Consuelo was an expert
on broken bones, so she did a report on it for her class at
school one day. As usual, she was behind in grades and
hoped to get a quick A. After explaining the different
kinds of breaks and the proper way to set bones, she went

over to the classroom door. When she was sure she had everyone's full attention, she slammed the heavy door closed on her forearm and pulled back hard. When the bone broke it made a loud snap, which was followed by the thud of her teacher fainting and the shrieks and gasps of her fellow students."

Everyone looked at Consuelo, who glanced up from her food and shrugged. Lydia liked telling the story and didn't get many opportunities.

"Of course she got in big trouble for that one, and afterwards we learned not to draw attention to ourselves."

The fly circled in for a landing. The two youngest sisters both shot hands out and made a grab at the fly. It happened so fast that Brad dropped a piece of fish off his fork.

Josephine slowly opened her hand, but there was no fly. Consuelo grinned big and squeezed her fist so hard it cracked. She opened her hand, but it too was empty.

"Ahem, looking for this?" Lydia opened her hand and an injured fly tried to fly away but landed on the table.

Lydia picked up the fly with a piece of tissue and deposited it in the trash on the way to the sink to wash her hands. She continued to her dumbfounded audience.

"Besides martial arts and survival, Logan knew a few magic tricks. But not as many as our mother's other friend."

Lydia had won the bet, of course. Jeremy had fallen again earlier that evening, all the way off the roof and onto the ground the second time. Actually some Crotons planted alongside the porch broke his fall. It was getting dark when he'd swatted at an early mosquito, slipped on some fresh tar, and did a roller.

Maybe sprained an ankle that time. Between the ankle, the scrapes on his stomach, and the sore legs from carrying all that stuff up the ladder, he wasn't feeling too hot.

He hadn't realized how much roofing tar he had gotten on himself until he took a shower. Soap didn't have much affect on the tar, but at least the purple blotches were starting to wear off.

The worst was, since he didn't get done, he was going to have to go back up the next day. He thought he should maybe go to the emergency room and get his ankle checked by a real doctor. Josephine said it was just a slight sprain, but what did she know? If not the emergency room, then at least go straight to bed and get some rest and keep weight off his sore ankle.

Jeremy gave all this some serious thought as he was going out the door, heading for the Pink Snapper.

☙

Lydia told Brad about their other teacher, an eccentric and powerful woman named Wiola. As she spoke, Brad thought he saw Josephine giving her oldest sister some kind of covert hand signals. Sign language?

"We were afraid of her at first, but our mother insisted we spend time with this woman. She would go into a trance and scare the bejesus out of us. Sit there with her eyes back up in her head with just the whites showing."

Brad was hanging on her every word.

"We finally got used to it though, and in fact that was one of the things she taught us."

Brad glanced at the other two women. They were looking down at their plates, but together slowly looked up at him with only the whites of their eyes showing.

"Holy shit!" Brad jumped back in his seat and dropped his fork.

Consuelo and Josephine did a slow blink and their eyes looked normal again. They were giggling like little girls. Lydia was not amused.

"Please excuse the childish behavior of my sisters, Brad. They have an immature sense of humor sometimes." The look she was giving her sisters was scaring him almost as much as the white-eyes thing had. Lydia suddenly smiled big and continued with her story.

"Wiola taught us each different things. I learned some magic tricks, Josephine got her start in alchemy, and Consuelo learned about men."

All eyes went to Consuelo who smiled modestly, then worked her eyebrows up and down suggestively.

"Our teachers taught us a lot of other things too. Practical things to help us take care of ourselves in the real world. They took us on field trips to places like hospitals, garages, and jails. We learned first-aid, what it's like to be blind or deaf, basic car repair, con games, disguises, and how to fight dirty. Sadly, we haven't seen or heard from our teachers since our mother died last year. I guess they decided we were ready to be on our own."

Brad was at a loss as to what to say. As strange as the story sounded, he was sure everything Lydia had told him was the truth. They continued eating in silence, and Brad noticed the three women finished their food at exactly the same time he did. Lydia clapped her hands together softly and smiled.

"Now, who wants pie?"

*   *   *

That was some good pie too, Josephine brought
me a little piece that evening. She lay on her
bed without any clothes on and read while I sat
between these two big, soft, warm pillows she
has on her chest, and ate pie. She read poetry
to me for a while and then got that look in her
eye that meant a quick trip across the street for
a ripe mango. Luckily, I had foreseen that
coming and had one rolled up under the bed
already. If you've never had a mango tongue
bath, you don't know what you're missing.

Chapter 6
The Artist

The sky threw a party and invited all its friends. The birds showed up early, as usual, flying around and squawking about the weather. The sun made an appearance but remained aloof, preferring to look down on the rest of the guests. Some white puffy clouds showed up fashionably late and mingled easily, laughing and telling jokes. They were the life of the party. The trees were pissed and just stood around on the ground pretending not to care that they hadn't been invited.

Miss Doris, fully abloom in freshly purchased floral prints and colorful scarves, found him on a sunny morning while taking one of her first strolls around the island. He was drawing a mural with charcoal on the side of a

house. It was quite an impressive mural of one of the early
Dali paintings. The young artist would tell her he could
see paintings in his mind as clearly as the first time he
saw them in art books. He hinted that he'd spent many
hours in libraries and art galleries stoned to the gills on
psychedelics.

A small crowd had formed that morning, watching the
eccentric young man who'd been drawing on sidewalks,
trashcans, buildings, and even trees for the past few days.
Miss Doris was a patron of the arts herself and recognized
the talent he possessed. Living alone in a house she'd
rented recently on the edge of Old Town, she'd just
turned 50 but was still young enough to fully appreciate
more than just the most obvious talents of the young
artist.

Miss Doris coaxed him away from the scene just as the
owner of the house was going into a full red-faced rage over
the surrealistic drawing on the side of his newly renovated
cigar-maker's house. She took him home and tried to
explain the ways of the world to the young man with the
wild eyes.

"My naughty Dali, you should be more careful. People
can be fun, but they can be dangerous too. Understand?"

Orange Dali looked up from the food she had set out for
him. He acted like he hadn't eaten in days — a true starving
artist.

"I hear voices in my head." He tapped his temple before
going back to his sandwich.

"I see. They tell you to draw on houses?" She was sitting
across the kitchen table, trying to see inside those eyes.

"No, of course not, that would be crazy. The voices tell
me to pick up bread, or that the kid got in trouble again, that

the check is in the mail, the estimate for the car was more than expected, and sometimes, just before they stop, the voices tell me they love me."

By the third sandwich, Miss Doris had learned that Orange Dali thought he might have been in a research experiment of some kind that involved implantable cell-phones. Something had obviously gone wrong.

"Where do you come from, my dear Dali? Where were you before you came here?"

He had found a container of potato salad in the fridge. She gave him a spoon. He gave her a blank look. "I really don't remember. I just come here for the season."

"Ah, the tourist season. So you can sell your artwork to tourists?"

He gave her an incredulous look and a little shake of his head. "No, I don't care about tourists. I'm here for the hurricane season." He looked at the fridge. "Can I have some of that pie?"

Miss Doris took good care of her new friend whenever he came around after that, and more than once they spent the night in her bed. But Miss Doris soon found out it was best to let him come and go as he pleased. He was quite the mad artist and not ready to be domesticated.

Orange Dali spent a lot of time watching the world go by from his secret spot next to a bike rack in Old Town. In the morning the spot was in the shade from a T-shirt shop, and in the afternoon the intense sun was behind a big tree across the street.

"Oh my, did you see his eyes? I bet there isn't a thought in that poor man's head!"

Orange Dali heard a lot of that from the tourists passing by. Of course he had thoughts, but most of them were very old thoughts. He had new thoughts too, usually about art, but sometimes about the weather or Miss Doris.

He wasn't really hidden very well sitting in his secret spot on the busy street. Sometimes he would hold a palm frond to help him blend in, but usually he just held very still, hoping no one would notice. It was important not to be noticed. People tended to act different if they thought no one was watching.

A man with long, tangled hair on a faded bicycle rode by. "Hey, OD!"

It was one of the local barflies, probably out during the light of day to hustle some tourists for a semi-honest buck. He didn't move or acknowledge the man, didn't want anyone to notice him. He wished he had a palm frond to hide behind.

A pale young couple speaking German walked by holding hands and looking hung-over. They stopped talking and stared at him as they walked by. He had decided to use his hat and orange cape to hide himself, but it didn't seem to work on Germans.

Another couple, these both males, not as young but just as pale, strolled by, gawking and whispering. They were looking at everything, just off one of the cruise ships.

"Oh my God! Look at that! Take my picture next to this creature!"

One of the strollers carefully stood next to the still and huddled form wrapped in orange plastic. The big-faced Swatch on the man's wrist hung down directly in Orange Dali's face. The ringing started in his head and the watch began to melt. His body shook with each ring, and he carefully slipped a hand out from under the cape and popped himself a good one on the side of the head. The watchwearer jumped back to his friend's side, and the ringing in the artist's head finally stopped completely as they walked away.

"H-hello."

It was the delicious dark-haired young woman from the old hotel. She was standing right in front of him, smiling. She had very intriguing eyes. He could tell she could see him, so there was no sense trying to hide. He tilted his hat back and gave her a little smile of his own.

"Have you s-s-seen this w-woman? It's s-someone who was around h-here a few m-months ago."

The image of the melting watch was burning in his brain and he needed to get it out. He took the picture from the babe with the big dark eyes and turned it over. With the picture on the ground, he produced a pen and furiously drew the image of the melting wristwatch on the back. When he was done, he handed it to the beauty and sat back on his spot. As she was giving his drawing a drop-jaw look, he noticed the picture of the woman.

"No, never seen her before. Sorry." Suddenly overcome with self-consciousness, he hid behind his hat and cape again.

"Y-you're a bit of a-a-an odd one!"

He peeked out at her and she gave him a wink.

"N-nice drawing. C-can I k-keep it?"

He buried his head deeper and waved his hand to dismiss any notion that he would want the picture. He'd only wanted to get it out of his head.

"T-thanks, I g-gotta go. B-bye!"

He snuck a look as she walked away. Thinking about those eyes. There was a man in a new car parked across the street watching her too. Something wasn't right about the man.

*   *   *

Josephine, my love, showed me a picture she got from the crazy street person with the funny mustache. Guy could draw; you got to give him that. She put it on the wall with some tape on one of the few spots on the wall that didn't already have a picture, map, chemistry diagram, or movie poster. She's got this one poster called E.T. with this weird little dude who looks a little like my cousin Ernie237. She told me about the movie one night. Sounded like a real yawner to me.

Chapter 7
The Beach

*The sun didn't show up for work the next
day. Didn't even call in. Swore it would never
go to another party. Getting too old for that
stuff. Slept all day and some dark clouds
from down south had to cover. The clouds
were so upset about the short notice they
couldn't be bothered with raining.*

Louie watched the hot little number walk away from the
freak with the orange cape. He'd dropped Gustov at the
beach a couple of hours earlier and tried to find a parking
place where he could keep an eye on things. Parking was a
real bitch in this town. He'd moved the car once, but it was
still in a lousy spot in the sun. He was sweating like a pig
and his jock itch was coming back. What a shit job this was
turning out to be.

To top it off, Gustov was being a real pain in the ass. Didn't want to help with the surveillance thing, said he'd be ready to do his part when it was time to go to work. Moody fucker. Just watched the Weather Channel in the motel room and fed the birds out at the beach. If it wasn't for the man's reputation, he'd make Gus for some kind of fucking weirdo.

It was the best beach in Key West, but it still wasn't all that much. Gustov grew up in the Miami area — now those were some beaches. Miles of sandy beach and blue water. It was a little odd in Miami these days, the way the towering condos and hotels shaded the beach in the afternoon; holiday weekends the place was a zoo, but it was still the best in the state.

When he was a kid, there was always a big day at the beach every weekend. Sundays the old man was at the Dolphins game or camped out in front of the tube, but Saturdays were beach day. His mom would make all kinds of food, they'd load the station wagon with every kind of beach shit known to man, and head out early. Most of the time they'd meet up with some friends or family, then turn the kids loose while the adults sat back and ate, drank, talked, and yelled at the kids.

It wasn't a bad deal unless you didn't like the beach. Of all the things Gus was afraid of as a child, most of them seemed to be at the beach in large numbers.

When he was little he was terrified of the seagulls. Winged sea rats, screeching and shitting everywhere, jumping on any little scrap of food dropped on the beach. One summer his parents got a new camera, and to use up the last of the film, they decided to get some pictures of their wimpy kid. It was some big family thing at the beach that day, and some of his older girl cousins were throwing Fritos up over their heads for the seagulls to catch.

The first six-pack of beer Gus's dad drank that day helped him decide to get the little wuss to overcome his fear of the stupid birds by holding a Frito over his head for the picture. Gus wasn't having any of it until his dad swatted him in the head and stuck his angry beer and fried chicken scented face up close.

"Quit being such a little baby in front of your cousins and do it!"

Gus looked to his mother for help, but she was setting her bottomless glass of rum-punch in the shade and picking up the camera, "Do what your father tells you!"

Gus stood over by the water with his eyes tightly closed, crying, and holding a Frito over his head with seagulls descending on him from all directions. Two birds made a pass at the same time. One grabbed the prize and some finger, and the other put a wing in his face.

His eyes popped open and he shrieked. His girl cousins started laughing their heads off. When he realized he'd wet his pants, he ran into the water. It was too late though — the moment had been captured on film for posterity. For years it was the hit of the family photo album for every houseguest who visited.

He finally got even with his dad.

The old man had gut cancer and it was either that or the drinking was going to kill him soon enough anyway. Gus spent a few years after that getting his room and board from the state and his continuing education from his fellow inmates. By the time he got out of prison he was seriously warped, but he had grown into a big man and there wasn't much he was afraid of anymore. Before long he was doing contract collections for a Miami businessman named Joey Thumbs.

There were seagulls on the beach in Key West, and some kids were throwing crackers. Gustov was wearing his usual slacks and sport shirt, watching from a picnic table in the shade. After the kids left he took a paper bag out of his pocket and threw a few handfuls up in the air. By the third throw, there were enough birds that not much was hitting the sand. When the bag was empty he called his partner on the cellphone. Dinner time, his treat.

"I'm gonna make the call."

Gustov got up and went to the pay phone just outside the restaurant. The man didn't like you to call him from a cellphone. Funny that way.

Louie headed for the can. He'd been needing to make a trip to the men's room and get cleaned up since his partner told him the story about the time some broad had cut out on a guy from one of the big families up north.

Bitch had grabbed not only a tidy sum of the family's cash, but a diary the guy's wife had been keeping. Said it was one of your more incriminating documents, and she was going to sell it to the newspapers if anyone fucked with her. Turns out she had some boyfriend on the side too, and they'd headed to Miami. Hide out there for a while.

Gustov got the job. Said it took him a couple days to find out where they were staying. Little apartment a couple blocks from the beach. Nice place. Kitchen with all your modern appliances for a carefree life. Stuck the boyfriend's hand down the garbage disposal till she came up with the diary. Boyfriend wasn't much, bled to death right there over the sink. Woman was so distraught she shot herself in the back of the head twice and jumped off a bridge into Biscayne Bay.

Louie didn't need to hear about that kind of shit. Very unsanitary thing, bleeding to death like that in the kitchen. He was having enough trouble getting to sleep these days as it was without thinking about some big piece of work like Gustov sticking some little screamer's hand down a garbage disposal.

While Gustov was making the call, he went to the restroom and soaped his hands up real good. He'd lost his appetite during the telling of the story but ate the steak anyway. He didn't want his partner to know the effect the story had on him. The steak wasn't setting too good in his stomach. He gave his hands another quick one, then splashed some water on his face before going back out to the table.

"You fall in or something? I was about to go in there looking for you." Gustov was smiling, so Louie figured he must have gotten good news. "I hope you remembered to wash your hands."

The big guy was Mr. Good Humor for once. Louie looked at the desert menu. Maybe a little bowl of ice cream to settle his stomach.

The big man dropped his voice. "It looks like it might be a go. We'll know for sure by tomorrow."

Gustov motioned to a waiter and leaned in a little closer. "This should be a nice easy job. I'd like to do some more of this kind of work, so let's make sure there aren't any problems, okay?"

Louie didn't like the way his partner was looking at him, shot him the look right back. They gave the waiter their dessert order, then went back to it. The only thing he'd been told when he signed on was if the job moved past the surveillance phase, the pay scale went up considerably. Gustov had filled him in a little more a couple days earlier. Just a little.

"So, we making a grab, or what?"

The big man waved it off.

"Patience. You know all you need to know at this point."

This kind of bullshit wasn't making Louie a happy man. It also wasn't helping his digestion either. This was the first time the two had worked together, even though they both did most of their work for the same man. Gustov seemed to enjoy keeping him just a little on edge. Must be the bully in him.

"I will tell you this. From what the boss was saying, it's got something to do with a real estate scam. Real big-time stuff."

*   *   *

Jeremy spends a lot of time trying to figure out a way to make a quick buck. He got enough money together forging lottery tickets to buy a computer so he could start an electronic chain letter on the Internet. A few days later he started getting money in the mail. He was real happy.

One day some big suits came in his room and showed him some shiny badges in wallets. They took Jeremy's computer, money, and Jeremy with them. The only thing left on his desk was the beer he'd been drinking. A little while later Jeremy came back and sat at his desk and looked real unhappy. I felt so sorry for him I almost wished I hadn't peed in his beer.

Chapter 8

Taco Bob

The sky was feeling a little under the weather. Maybe it was just gas, or one of those 24-hour bugs. Something down there just didn't feel right. Might as well just tough it out; when you're the sky you can't call in sick. It wasn't helping matters any with the sun showing up all bright-eyed and rested after a day off.

Josephine slipped the piece of fur in the pocket of her shorts when she saw Lydia walking toward the front desk.

"Did the Morgans come in yet? I expected them in here this morning. Hope they aren't going to be another no-show."

"C-called. Be here t-tonight. D-driving down from Mi-Miami. Rented a c-convertible."

Lydia picked up the stack of mail from behind the desk for a look. "Can't say I blame them much, nice day for it. Not a cloud in the sky.

"Here's another letter from our friends at MegaDrug. Sure are some persistent bastards. I thought maybe they'd get the picture when I called and made it very clear we weren't selling."

Josephine finished what she was doing on her laptop and shut the computer down. She didn't stutter on the Internet. Lydia started through the rest of the mail and plopped down in the chair behind the desk as soon as her sister stood up. Shift change.

"You going to check on your patient? I looked in on him an hour ago and he seemed to be resting quietly. Of course, that was after I took his head out of the toilet and drug him back over to the bed. Your latest batch of hangover remedy doesn't seem to be quite ready for the general public, if you ask me. That is unless several hours of the dry heaves is supposed to be part of the cure."

Josephine smiled. "I m-make it a little s-stronger when I t-try it out on J-Jeremy. See if t-there's any s-side effects."

"Well, just try not to kill him. Okay?"

Josephine stuck out her lower lip and was about to go into a pout when the front door opened. A tall, thin, weathered-looking man dressed like a sport fisherman and wearing a cowboy hat came in.

"Afternoon, ladies." The man tipped his hat as he came over to the front desk. "Ya'll the ones left this picture at my houseboat a few days ago?"

The sisters looked at each other, then at the picture the man put on the desk before shaking their heads no.

"It might have been our sister Consuelo, she's been working the marina area. Have you seen the person in the picture?"

The man took off his hat and scratched his head a little. "Well, I might know her, but I'd be interested in knowing how ya'll come to be looking for her."

The man had the full attention of the two women. Lydia set the stack of mail down and Josephine put her laptop on a shelf behind the desk. They were ready.

"That's our older sister. We're pretty sure she was here in Key West a few months ago, but no one's seen her since. We lost touch with her years ago and ..."

The front door burst open. Consuelo stomped in with a tanned young man slung over her shoulder. She kicked the door closed ignoring her sisters and the fisherman and headed for her room with a determined look in her eyes. The young man looked up as they passed and gave a shy smile and a little shrug.

"Consuelo!"

Not even a break in her stride, she just kept on stomping through the lobby. Lydia tried again.

"Consuelo, it's important."

She stopped and turned slowly. Her face was flushed and there was fire in the eyes that had gone cat-like.

"It's about Sara. Just tell your little friend you'll play with him later."

Consuelo grudgingly walked back towards the front door and dropped the young man on one of the couches in the lobby. She gave him a long lick on the face, then laid him down and covered him with cushions from the other sofa. When she was sure her snack was safe from other predators, she came over and stood facing the others with her arms crossed. "This better be good. I got plans."

"Yes dear, we can see that." Lydia rolled her eyes. "I believe this man was about to tell us something about Sara when you returned from safari."

The fisherman was taking it all in, but he was smiling.

"Name's Taco Bob, ladies. I been out fishing a few days, and when I came back there was this picture with the phone number on it. I did a little asking around, then came by here."

Consuelo picked up on it. "Okay, yeah, I left that with some guy on a houseboat. What have you got for us? Have you seen our sister?"

"I ain't seen her in a while, but I do know her. I asked some mutual friends if they seen her lately, but she's been gone like y'all said, for a while now." He obviously realized this wasn't playing too good. "I kinda got a hunch where she might be though."

∞

Louie couldn't believe what he just saw. Some little blond number just walked in the hotel with a guy over her shoulder like he was a stuffed toy. Guy must have had 40 pounds on her at least. This was some kind of crazy town. No wonder people called it Key Weird.

Last time he was in town on business was a pretty simple job. One of those new Internet companies for losers who want to get even came up with some work.

Some asshole really pissing you off on the net? You can send a pointed email, or if you got a gold card, you can send someone like Louie to deliver a personal message. Louie liked the way it worked. Company gives you an address, half the money up front, and usually a picture of the one getting the attention.

Job was a breeze. Found the guy — fucker was up in the middle of the night on the net, as usual. Knock on the door. Guy won't open up — he's a real smart guy. Tell him you're the police, Detective Brown, someone seen prowling around the area, just checking to make sure everyone's all right. Door opens. Drop a sap on the guy's head and he lays on the floor so you can break his fingers one at a time with a ball-peen hammer. Neat. Clean. Guy gets the message not to use his keyboard for a while. Everybody's happy.

At least he got a decent parking space for a change. Sitting in the heat with no air-conditioning was playing hell with his heat rash though. Wasn't a cloud in the sky either, usually some kind of clouds in the afternoon, get a little break from the sun. Gustov said it looked like they should be getting the word anytime. Louie was ready for some action.

After some further introductions, Taco Bob gave the three sisters a rundown on what he knew about Sara's past, which wasn't really all that much, he realized. That she had once been in the same cult as a lady friend of his was still a little unsettling for him.

"First time I laid eyes on her was way on back up in the Everglades swamp. She was staying in a little cabin and poling around in one of those dugout canoes like the Indians used to have around there. Acted like she been doing it all her life."

The sisters looked a little uncomfortable with this and were trading glances. He noticed they were also giving each other little covert signs with their hands and feet. Consuelo went over to the couch and dug up her new friend. She whispered in his ear and he slipped out the door smiling. The taller one who seemed to be in charge, named Lydia, waited for her sister to rejoin them.

"Excuse me for asking, but how did you happen to be back up in that swamp yourself?"

"I was looking for a old fella used to live in a cabin there, but he was gone. Sara said she hadn't seen hide nor hair of him either."

After sending her friend away, the one called Consuelo was standing off to the side, so he had to look away from the other two women to keep an eye on her. It was making it harder to notice their covert signals. Consuelo jumped in next.

"So you think she's still out there in the swamp? That was the last time you saw her?"

"No, actually she followed me on back to Key West in her skiff. Last time I seen her was here on the island the evening we came back."

'She had her own skiff? Like a powerboat?" The little blonde looked like she couldn't believe it. "We've done a lot of things, but never tried to run a powerboat over open water like that. Are you sure?"

"Yep. Seemed to handle it pretty good too. I reckon she had some expert instruction." He gave a big wink, but the women were so busy all trying to sign to each other at the same time that none of them seemed to notice. Except Josephine.

"W-where do you th-th-think S-Sara is then?"

Taco Bob was a little taken aback that the dark-haired beauty had such a bad stutter. "Oh, I wouldn't be surprised if she didn't go on back up there in the swamp again. She kinda seemed to like it there."

Josephine frowned big. She obviously didn't like the idea of her older sister wanting to live in a swamp.

"W-why was s-s-she in t-the s-swamp?"

He didn't really want to get into telling these young ladies their long-lost sister might be a few ants short of a picnic.

"I reckon you might want to ask her about all that if you meet up with her your own self. She's got her own ideas about some things." He got a little smile started up for the sisters. "I can tell you this though, the last I seen her it looked like she was going to be doing all right financially."

As he thought it would, this started off a whole new set of subtle signing between the young women.

"Actually, I been wanting to take a ride up there again sometime, see if I could maybe find out something about my old friend who used to live up there." There was a flurry of foot movements and hand signs. "Weren't for this big storm coming, I might could be talked into taking a look tomorrow. Probably want to wait a few days now though."

The signals between the sisters stopped. All three stared right at him and said in unison, "What storm?"

∞

Jeremy was watching the Weather Channel in his room in the back of the hotel. He had recovered sufficiently to turn on the television on his way back from his latest trip to the bathroom. Now he was lying in bed trying to decide if it was worth the effort to find the remote so he could change the channel. He needed to tell Josephine to go a little easy on the jalapeño peppers in her hangover remedy next time.

He wouldn't be surprised if his farts didn't eventually burn
a hole in his underwear.

He peeked out of the sheets when he heard the guy on
the tube saying something about a tropical storm. There was
some weather geek, who looked like he spent way too much
time sitting around indoors, pointing at a swirl of colors
down below Cuba. Guy was talking about Florida and saying something about a possible Hurricane Watch while trying to cover his ass with the usual jive about computer mod-
els. The time lapse thing made it look like it was heading for
Florida all right.

Jeremy decided this could be some serious shit and
probably required immediate and sustained action on his
part in preparing for the storm. Not to mention the opportunities for ducking out of work and scamming a buck or two.

He was sound asleep before the next commercial.

There was a little television in the lobby. Taco Bob and
the three sisters were sitting in front of it, waiting for the
Tropical Storm Report to come around. He was offered something to drink but declined politely. Consuelo brought him a
beer anyway when she came back with one for herself.

"Thanks. I was just telling your sisters here, the reports
I seen earlier had this coming over Cuba and getting on up
to hurricane strength. Them folks is wrong on these storms
a lot, but if it gets to being a bad one and comes this way,
there's gonna be a lotta folks wanting to get outta Dodge
here all of a sudden. Those few staying are gonna be mighty
busy with getting their property ready for the blow." He took
a long pull on his beer. "It ain't the best of times for a boat
ride either."

The storm report came on and said the storm had slowed its forward movement but was now a hurricane. Hurricane Watches were expected to be issued for the Keys and points north within 24 hours. The sisters knew about hurricanes but never had to deal with one before. Consuelo killed her beer and crumpled the can while she walked over to the window.

"Sure doesn't look like any storm's coming. There isn't a cloud in the sky."

"Yep, from what I seen, storm kinda pulls all the clouds down to it like that sometimes. I imagine you take a good look down south from here, you might see the edge of some serious looking weather."

Consuelo was still by the window. "I'd go take a look from the widow's walk, but we don't have one."

Lydia dismissed that with a wave of her hand and looked Taco Bob in the eye.

"What if this storm goes into the Everglades? If Sara's there, I wouldn't imagine a little cabin in the swamp is going to be very safe."

She had a point.

"No, I don't reckon it would be. Of course I got no way of knowing if she went on back to the 'Glades, or if she's there now." He was giving it some thought. "That skiff she had was a rental. It might be a good idea to ask them folks at the boat rental place just this side of the big marina if they know anything."

Everyone looked at Consuelo.

"I was there showing Sara's picture, but I didn't get anything. Maybe I'll give it another try. Like right now." She started for the door, then stopped. "Come on, Bugs, I got an idea."

The two young women were out the door without another word.

The head meteorologist came on the television with the latest projection — looked like the hurricane was going to continue north and cross Cuba in the next 48 hours. The guy mentioned Key West is only 90 miles from Cuba.

When the report was over, Taco Bob looked away from the television. Lydia wasn't saying anything but was looking at him. He knew what the look meant.

"We'll see what your sisters find out down at the boat rental place. If it's going to happen, it's going to have to be early on, first thing tomorrow morning, and hopefully get back before dark. Looks like the water's going to be rough as a cob after that, and I ain't wanting to be riding out no storms in the 'Glades." He got a slow nod from Lydia. "I reckon one of ya'll is going to want to go along if I'm not mistaken."

The sisters got a cab to the marina. Consuelo remembered the fat Cuban woman working there from when she'd passed through before. She showed the picture to her again.

"No, sorry, honey. I don't remember seeing her."

"Her name's Sara. She might have rented a boat here a few months ago."

"Oh, well, I've only been here for —"

"Anyone else here? Someone who might have been around a few months ago?"

Both sisters were giving the woman their full-intensity stares now. The big woman made a break for the manager's office.

The manager was a big dark man in his '40s with a shoe-brush moustache. Coming out the door, he looked pissed about being disturbed but brightened when he saw two good-looking young women standing in his showroom of seriously marked-up marine supplies. Maybe thought he had some hot little vacationers needing some personal instruction on one of the rentals. His smile faded when he got close.

"We're looking for this woman. She may have rented a boat from here a few months ago."

He took a good look at the picture that was held up to him, then at the two young women staring intensely at him. He took a step back. A quick flash of something in his eyes. Fear.

He put the smile back on, but to Consuelo he read guilty of every crime known to man.

"Sorry girls, I haven't ... ."

Holding the picture in front of the manager's chest, Consuelo came to his side and whispered softly, "Look again. Maybe you'll remember."

He looked at the picture in her hand. When he looked up, Josephine was on her toes and in his face. He started to say something about not seeing anyone who — but there was more whispering in his ear.

"Doesn't she have interesting eyes? Very deep eyes I would say. You could go very far down in those eyes." He started to nod just as Consuelo slipped behind him and softly put an iron lock on his head with the palms of her hands while gently holding his eyelids open with her fingers.

"Just relax and look into those soft eyes. Can you feel it?"

She knew what it was like to look into her sister's eyes. Two pools of black liquid pulling you into a void that slowly filled with an almost physical presence of pure fear that probed your body, searching, until it was inside you and then started to eat its way back out.

When he started a low, trembling wail, Consuelo began to whisper again.

"The woman in the picture was here, wasn't she? Where is she now?"

The man said something that sounded like, "please." They sat him in a chair. He had his hands over his face and looked up for just a second when some knuckles popped him on the top of his head.

"She bought one of my rental boats from me a few months ago. I don't know who she is or where she went."

Josephine looked at her sister and shrugged. Consuelo wanted more.

"Why didn't you just tell us that? There must be something else."

The man was crying now; he wouldn't take his hands from his face.

"She paid me for the boat with Spanish treasure. Gold coins."

The back door opened and the fat woman came in, followed closely by a sun-scorched man with a mean leer and a big wrench.

"They're doing something to Rudy! I think they're trying to rob him!"

The lug made a swing at Consuelo with the wrench. She grabbed the wrench with one hand, some wrist with the other, and spun the big guy toward the front door. Police officer Thomas Sanchez, responding to the disturbance call, opened the door just in time to see the little blonde throwing a couple hundred pounds of outboard mechanic at him. Both men went down hard.

☙

Lydia picked Josephine up at the police station a couple of hours later, but it looked like Consuelo was staying put for a while for assaulting a police officer with a mechanic. Luckily, other than some bruised male egos, no one was hurt.

Lydia called Brad, who knew a good lawyer. There was nothing else Lydia or Josephine could do. The cops were all upset because one of their own had taken a fall. The sisters decided to let the lawyer take a shot at it. At least he was used to dealing with these people.

Taco Bob had gone back to his houseboat before Lydia had gotten the call. He had to get his floating home ready for the storm and make sure everything was set in case he was making an early morning run up to the Everglades. Lydia had offered to pay him for taking Consuelo along, but he had come up with the polite refusal thing again.

But things had changed; Consuelo wasn't going anywhere for a while. Lydia would go herself, but she couldn't see Josephine dealing too effectively with the world of cops and lawyers. Not to mention running a hotel full of people who were liable to panic if the hurricane got any closer. She called Brad.

"Hey, Brad, it's me. Could you possibly cover for me here at the hotel for a couple hours tomorrow morning? I need to meet your lawyer friend and see if I can get Consuelo out of there."

"We've got a meeting at the office in the afternoon about this storm, but I could probably come by for an hour or two in the morning before I go in."

"Thanks, I really appreciate this, Brad. I'll make it up to you somehow." She had a real good idea of how she'd like to make it up to him but was much too busy at the moment for pleasant thoughts.

When Lydia called Taco Bob next and passed along the information about Sara buying a boat, he agreed it was looking like she might have gone back to the swamp. She didn't see any need to bother him with any details about Consuelo's arrest, just assured him he would have a passenger.

She had to deal with a pouting Josephine next.

Josephine was still upset about the cops hauling off her sister. The handcuff thing had brought her to tears, and she was still in a state when Lydia found her in her room.

"Buck-up, Josey! We'll get her out, don't worry."

Lydia knew just the thing to get her to stop dwelling on the whole sister-in-jail thing.

"How would you like to take a nice boat ride tomorrow with that fisherman who was here? Get out in the air! See some new things! Hang out in a mosquito-plagued swamp! Maybe find our sister Sara! What do you say?"

Josephine was lying on her bed holding something to her chest that Lydia couldn't see. She rolled over a little but didn't say anything, just frowned horribly.

"Look Josephine, she could be hurt or something. She might need someone who would know how to help her." She sat on the bed next to her sister. "I'm sure you'll be all right, Taco Bob seems to know what he's talking about, and we need to find out if Sara's out there before this storm comes."

Josephine started to come around.

"I n-n-need to get s-some stuff ready."

She wasn't exactly smiling, but Lydia could tell her sister was already thinking about what she would need for her trip to the swamp. Josephine loved to pack all kinds of strange little things in her traveling bag.

"Go ahead and get your stuff packed and try to get some sleep. Tomorrow's shaping up to be a big day."

*   *   *

Josephine finally let go of me when her sister left. Good thing too, she was about to hug the stuffing out of me. She got out a backpack and started putting some of her potions and medicines and stuff in there.

I offered to go along but she said it might be dangerous — snakes, sharks, alligators, big spiders, that kind of stuff. The spiders thing did it for me. I helped her pack and told her a story about the Blue Planets of Sirus 3 to help her get to sleep.

Chapter 9

The Grab

*Something was in the air. The clouds all left
town in a huff, and the birds were taking a
long lunch. Only the trees stood their ground.
The breeze was acting suspicious, and the
sun was getting everyone hot under the
collar.*

Taco Bob knew the storm was still a long ways away, but
the water already looked different than usual in the first light
of day. Flat seas with low undulating swells, and not much
sign of fish or birds.

He didn't even want to think about getting out on the
water and having a problem that left him out there with a
storm coming. There'd been a bad experience with thunderstorms on a trip to the Glades once before, and that was
enough to make a believer out of him. He'd already checked
everything on the boat twice by the time the sisters arrived.

"Morning, ladies. I reckon I got things purty well squared away here. You want to come on aboard, we'll be heading out."

The question of which one was coming with him was settled when the dark-haired one with the stutter stepped aboard his skiff and had a seat. He stowed her bulging back-pack in the forward hatch.

"You kids have a good time and don't stay out too late!"

Lydia was smiling big. Taco Bob was giving her a look and Josephine was giving her the finger. Lydia gave up on the smiling. "Jeez, lighten up you two. I was just trying to get some humor going here!"

She had her hands on her hips. Taco Bob turned loose a little smile before getting back to business.

"I got the number to the hotel, and you got my number, but I doubt this thing's going to be much good once we get out very far." He clipped a cellphone to his belt.

Lydia looked worried as he started the big outboard engine and pushed off from the dock.

Taco Bob eased the flats boat out of the marina, and they gave Lydia a final wave. He glanced at his passenger. "I kinda thought your other sister was the one coming along."

Josephine looked thrilled and scared shitless at the same time. She'd probably never been in a small powerboat before. The black-haired beauty shrugged.

"J-jail".

Taco Bob gave her a glance, then gave the engine full throttle. Josephine's eyes got big as she held on tight and let out a little squeal. The boat jumped up on a plane and they sped off toward the sun just coming up on the horizon.

∞

Lydia was in no mood to mess around. She went straight to Jeremy's room when she got back and dragged the still sleeping handyman out of bed and onto the hardwood floor.

"Ouch! Hey, what's the deal? Jesus Christ on Ice, Lydia, what are you doing?" Jeremy rubbed another bump on his head and pulled some sheet over his exposed private areas.

"Front desk in ten minutes, Jeremy. You're going to be earning your keep today." Ignoring the steady stream of whining coming from the floor, she headed for the front.

With the television in the lobby tuned to the weather, Lydia took a quick look at the newspaper while she waited for Jeremy. Last night's update on the storm was the main story for page one. She was reading about evacuation and storm preparedness when the Halls from Toronto came down to the lobby on their way to breakfast.

They exchanged the latest news and personal opinions about the storm. Then Mrs. Hall asked Lydia if she'd heard about the birds. She picked up the paper Lydia had been looking at.

"I bet there's something in here about it. Here it is, read this. They've been finding a lot of dead birds around the beach the last few days."

Orange Dali was doing a mural in chalk for a growing crowd on Duval Street. Miss Doris had surprised him with the colored pieces of chalk the night before. He hadn't shown any interest in the canvas she had set up in the study but had done a hauntingly lovely nude on the white sheet of her bed. In the morning they were both covered in chalk.

He'd tried several surfaces before he found one that the chalk liked that morning. He stood on an overturned bucket and created his signature soft watches on the side of a white panel truck. The driver of the truck had joined the crowd after his attempts to stop Dali had been booed down by the assembled throng of picture-taking tourists. There was even a cop car stopped around the corner, watching the impromptu art piece take form.

Louie was sweating his ass off. They'd gotten the go-ahead for the job, and it was going down in just a little while. Now there was a bunch of people staring at something happening around the other side of a truck a block over. Looked like a couple donut-eaters sitting in a cruiser watching whatever was going on. Occupational down-side. Cops always made him nervous, but if the fucks had to be around, he liked having them where he could see them.

He wasn't the only one sweating today. Plenty of soaked tourists wandering the streets bitching about the blazing hot sun. In a few hours they'll be packed like sardines at Mallory Square trying to get a glimpse of the same sun setting over the heads of several hundred other tourists. Louie decided he could miss that shit. Besides, things went right here, he'd soon be making some serious money just sitting on his ass in the air-conditioning.

Made one more stroll, and everything looked good as far as he could tell. He didn't one bit like Gustov having him do the street work out front while His Highness sat in their rental parked back in the alley. He could see a newspaper through the windshield. Here he was out doing the final recon while his partner sat on his fat ass and read the paper in the shade. That sucked.

❧

"Just make sure the storm shutters are all ready to go. You can do that, can't you, Jeremy?"

"Those hinges are going to be pretty rusty, Lydia. I probably need to get some hinge oil from the hardware store before I start."

She looked like she'd never heard of hinge oil before. Jeremy wasn't sure if he had either. Best he should ask the guys at the hardware.

"Okay, whatever. Just make sure those shutters are ready, then get that roof finished. Big day, Jeremy. Let's get something done for a change, shall we?"

He wasn't liking her attitude one bit. Had a lot of nerve to expect him to work on a day when he was so hung-over. Actually he realized he didn't feel all that bad, other than the latest lump on his head where he'd slipped in the bathroom. Maybe there was something to Josephine's latest cure.

"I think I might need some more roofing tar too."

Lydia looked up from what she was doing at the front desk.

"Just get whatever you need from the hardware. I'll be gone for a couple of hours this morning, but other than that, I'll be here all day."

❧

When Maria came in to clean rooms, Lydia went over a few things with her about the storm preparations. As usual, Jeremy's name came up.

"That man, he no good, Miss Lydia! I doon trust him no farther I can throw him!"

Lydia had heard it all before. She was so glad they only had two employees.

"Yes, Maria, you've made that abundantly clear to me in the past. But we still have to honor the agreement we made when we bought this place. Maybe he'll straighten up and be a model worker in the next few months."

Maria made a snorting sound and went off into the hotel muttering to herself.

The Pink Snapper Lounge wasn't exactly on the way to the hardware store, unless you took the scenic route. Jeremy hadn't really planned on stopping either, but the barback, Tony, was out front changing the sign when he went by.

"What's up, Tony?"

Tony was used to looking down on the short bald man, but up on the ladder he was really looking down on him.

"Besides me, not much, maggot. Nice bike, by the way."

Jeremy was puffing around on a rusty old bicycle with big wire baskets. He shrugged. "Company bike. Headed for the hardware."

He probably would have gone there too, if Tony hadn't said, "Boss's auditioning some new talent in there this morning. You outta go take a look."

At the same instant Jeremy was opening the door to the topless bar, the front door of the hotel opened and two men came in. The big one wearing slacks and a sport shirt and the smaller one in a suit wiping his hands with a little towel. They walked up to the front desk with the big one clearing his throat.

"Good morning. My associate and I are introducing a new insurance plan to selected businesses in this area. I've got one of our cards right here." The big guy pulled out a gun, set his feet, and shot Brad square in the neck.

Louie just about shit.

"What the fuck did you just do? We weren't supposed to shoot anybody here!"

He stared at the gun his partner was holding, then realized there were wires coming from the gun over to the guy on the floor. It was a stun gun, a taser. Gustov could have given him some warning here. The plan had been to use a sap if the mark didn't come along easy.

Louie went for a look and the guy was down but not completely out. Had two little darts on the end of the wires stuck to his neck. He looked over at Gustov standing there with a big shit-eating grin on his face.

Gustov always liked what the taser could do. Take your basic big, mean, drugged-out, barroom bruiser. Give him a shot and he's quivering mush on the floor. Overrides the nervous system with something like 50,000 volts. He liked to use it on women especially. Worked real good on females, the smaller the better.

"Quit your whining, Louie, and bring the car up to the side door. Like now." Louie started to say something, but just gave his partner a wary look and hurried out for the car.

*   *   *

While my Josephine was gone I worked in the lab on the hangover potion. My basic knowledge of Zertronian chemistry isn't much help with the limited ingredients available. It's mostly a matter of trial and error.

Our main test subject, Jeremy, sometimes has a problem with his skin turning yellow after drinking the potion, so I'm thinking about cutting back on the sulfur and cat urine.

Chapter 10
Sara

The air was thick with anticipation. The wind had been throwing its weight around down south but got stuck in weak high-pressure traffic and wasn't expected in till the late shift. Crews from the mainland swamps had worked all night, bringing in extra humidity for the still air. The sun and heat got into another senseless argument, and everyone was steamed by lunch.

Josephine had needed to pee for the last hour, so she was really glad when the boat slowed down as they came up on the coastline. It didn't look like what she'd expected though; miles of tall forest lined the edge of the land without a break. No buildings, or cars, or power lines even. Just solid trees. They'd seen a few other boats off in the distance on the long ride across Florida Bay, but not much else.

"I r-r-really got t-to pee!"

It wasn't looking good for a convenient and clean public restroom to be appearing anytime soon, or she wouldn't have said anything. Taco Bob told her they were coming into the channel for Lost Man's Creek. He cut the engine down to idle, but left it running in neutral, before handing her a plastic bucket and going to the front of the boat. The mangrove trees up ahead of the boat looked exactly the same as the ones for several miles in each direction, but he gave them a good look anyway.

After Josephine had made herself comfortable, they eased slowly up the creek. It was mid-morning, but the mosquitoes were after them anyway as soon as they got up into the tree canopy.

"Them's Red Mangrove trees, Josephine. There's lots of little creeks all along the coast coming outta the 'Glades and the whole area's thick with mangroves. So thick, not much else growing for a ways either."

Josephine was wondering how he had been able to tell where to go, when she noticed he was glancing at a little thing the size of a cell phone velcroed onto the center console of the boat. She pointed to it.

"GPS. Satellite thing for finding your way. One of your better ideas for boats in a long time. I got some positions last time I was up in here. Should get us up in there without getting lost so much."

He was right about the trees. Not much of any other vegetation growing up in there; the mangroves and their tangle of roots had a monopoly on that area of black mud, black water, and black mosquitoes.

It wasn't too bad while they were running in the boat, but as soon as they slowed down it got hot. The trees gave plenty of shade, but there wasn't a breath of breeze and the humidity was incredible. They were both sweating and swatting mosquitoes. They put on insect repellent and it helped a little with the bugs.

The bottom of the engine bumped something, and Taco Bob raised the engine up a little and kept on. Before long the creek was looking more like a lake full of trees, and he cut the engine off because it was hitting sunken logs down in the black water.

"I'm going to have to pole in from here on. It's pretty near low tide, and I don't want to be taking a chance on bending a prop back up in here." He got out the long pole fastened on the side of the boat and began pushing the boat back up further into the swamp. "I got a spare prop. In fact I got just about a spare everything somewhere on this boat, but I don't want to be doing no repair work today. Just hoping we can find the cabin, see what's up with anybody there, and get back. Not a good night to be camping out with that storm coming. We're needing to get in here and back out pretty quick."

Josephine nodded. She liked outdoors, nature, and all that crap, but she had no intention of spending the night out in any mosquito swamp.

"Here's us a gator!"

She looked where he was pointing up ahead and saw something about two feet long sticking up out of the water just a little. About the time she realized what she was looking at was only the head, the alligator seemed to decide the boat was getting too close and made a huge splash before disappearing under the water. Josephine was glad she'd used the bucket already.

"He won't bother us none. Most times people get hurt is when they're in the water. Never heard of one jumping in a boat." He gave Josephine a wink.

She was hoping that if Sara was back up in the swamp, she would have the decency to have her bags packed and be ready to go, immediately. She trusted Taco Bob, but she really wished Consuelo or Lydia had come along; she wasn't used to being so far from them. The thought brought a shiver, even in the heat.

"We should be coming up on the old cabin here before long."

☞

Consuelo was cooling her heels in the county slammer. She was "inside" and already a hardened member of the prison community.

"Hey, Molly, you gonna play cards, or what?"

Consuelo popped her chewing gum. She'd expected to have to fight some big bull dykes right away, or at least some crazy, pimp-eviscerating, crack whore would be after her with a knife made out of a spoon. Instead she was in a holding cell with Molly, a mousy 24 year-old kindergarten teacher from Detroit who'd come to Key West with a girl-friend and puked conch-fritter-flavored beer on the wrong cop's shoes outside Capt. Tony's bar the night before.

Molly didn't look too dangerous, she just looked very hung-over and miserable. Consuelo was feeling extra perky; she'd never been in jail before and was trying to make the best of it.

"One of my sisters is making a cure for hangovers. We figured with Key West having like about the most bars per capita in the US, it would be a great place to experiment."

Molly looked up with bloodshot eyes from the cards she was holding limply in her hand and moaned, "That's nice."

"You going to eat that?" Consuelo's sparkling blue eyes were locked on the baloney sandwich Molly was trying to avoid even looking at.

"Uh, no, help yourself."

Consuelo snatched up the sandwich and tore into it, sending a big bite down to join her own sandwich. Molly was looking a little green.

"I don't see how you can eat that!"

Consuelo pushed the rest of the sandwich in her mouth, chewed twice, swallowed, and belched.

"My body likes most everything! Wish I had a big glass of beer to wash that down with now." She gave her cellmate a big wink.

While Molly was dry heaving again in their toilet, Consuelo was tempted to check on her cellmate's cards. Old habit. But she decided since she'd already won most of Molly's money playing poker with the jail's 43-card deck, she'd let it go.

Sara was so weary. She'd been walking for days in the yellow world. The air was heavy with sulphur gas, and the yellow ground was soft, but there was no comfort here. She was so tired and just wanted a nice place to lie down.

From habit she looked at her hand and counted fingers. Definitely more than five, and rather withered and crooked as well. So she was still dreaming; it was a dream. She remembered that her body was lying on a mat in a little cabin in the swamp, and she was very sick. The shadow that had been following to the left was getting more noticeable. She knew now that it was the shadow of death and it was getting closer.

She stopped walking. There didn't seem to be much point in it; everything was just a murky, gassy, unpleasant shade of yellow. She noticed the ground was actually made up of soft little bubbles. She kicked at them, and several flew up slowly, with a sickening wobble. The bubbles were making her feel dizzy, so she grabbed one of the larger ones in front of her face to steady herself. The bubble grew larger and more transparent in her hand. She looked inside, but there was only yellow until she closed her eyes. Then she could see, not with her eyes, but with her entire being.

There was a flood of emotions and visions. Spectacular sights revealed themselves but were soon gone, leaving her with a curious feeling. There was still the nearly overwhelming need to rest, and her dark companion to the left seemed nearer than ever; but something was different. She summoned up all her strength to think and then knew what it was that was different. She had become so accustomed to being alone, it was somewhat of a shock. She had company.

"L-look at her!" Josephine was kneeling and crying her eyes out next to the gaunt figure on the mat. Her sister looked dead.

"Let me have a look here. She ain't doing too good all right. Musta got the fever."

Taco Bob put his hand on Sara's forehead. Her eyes fluttered a little but didn't open.

"Attagirl. You looking a little rough here, Sara. Can you talk?"

Josephine was in full wail now over her sister.

"She's probably dehydrated. All that crying ain't going to do her any good now, Josephine. You want to help your sister, see if you can get her to drink something while I try out this phone."

Josephine was having trouble getting it together. She got a plastic bottle of water out of her backpack and tried to get Sara to drink. She was still blubbering, and her hands were shaking so bad she was getting water all over her sister, but not in her.

She needed Lydia or Consuelo to help her calm down, like they always did when she got like this.

"S-s-shit!" She was so frustrated with herself, she was crying louder than ever. She threw the nearly empty bottle of water at the wall and slapped herself on the cheek, hard. The blow was such a shock it took her breath away. She shook her head and looked up and noticed some little roots tied to the rafters of the cabin.

"Feel better?"

It was a tiny whisper. Josephine looked down at her sister. Her eyes were open a little.

"Sara!"

Josephine hugged the bundle of rags that was her sister, and almost started crying again. She grabbed another bottle of water and helped Sara drink. She gagged on the water and started coughing just as Taco Bob came back inside.

"This phone ain't going to do us any good out here. I guess Lydia is gonna know we found her when we get back."

He knelt down by the two sisters just as Sara got over the coughing and made a loud fart.

"Atta girl, Sara! No need to show off for us though, you're going to have to try to save your strength." He was smiling, but he seemed worried. She did look bad. "See if you can get her to drink a little more of that water. We're doing good on time and I want to take a quick look around here before we start back."

Josephine didn't say anything. She just held her sister's head again so she could drink.

The little cabin with the mangrove trees grown up around it didn't look any different, but the boat Sara had bought in Key West was full of rainwater and mostly sunk in the shallow water by the little cabin. She'd either been sick for a while, or just didn't care about getting back out again someday. Inside the cabin, it didn't look like anyone had done any cooking with the little stove for a long time.

"Sara, we're going to carry you on out of here, take you back to Key West and get you well. Okay?"

Josephine had her stripped and was checking her over. Sara looked up at worried faces and tried to smile.

"S-she's really th-thin, but s-sound. I don't th-think she's eaten in w-w-weeks. M-must have s-starved out the f-f-fever."

After Josephine had cleaned her up a little and dressed her in some of the clothes she'd brought along, Taco Bob carried his sickly friend out to the boat. He'd made a makeshift bed in the bottom of the boat with the life jackets and blankets he had on board. As they tried to get her comfortable for the ride back in, Sara motioned to him to come close so she could whisper.

By the time he came back out of the cabin, the two sisters were as ready as they were going to be.

"I'm glad you remembered this, Sara. I'd forget just as sure."

He set a small, but heavy, dirt-gray bag down next to her. She smiled and gave him a slow wink. Josephine looked in the bag.

"G-g-gold!" She gave one of the long chains of heavy gold an astounded look.

"I told you she was doing all right financially. Not much to spend it on out here though."

Josephine checked out more of the contents of the bag while Taco Bob poled the boat back toward deeper water. It was all gold treasure.

"Y-you're rich! Wh-where?"

"I'm sure your sister will be glad to tell you the story when she gets to feeling better. Right now, we need to be concentrating on getting her, and us, back to civilization in one piece. That wind's coming up."

Though they couldn't feel much breeze in the dense mangrove swamp, up above they could see the tops of the trees moving. When they got out to where they could use the motor, Taco Bob showed Josephine how to operate the boat. There was going to be a lot of rough water, and he wanted her checked out on running the boat in case she needed to do something like turn around and get him if he went overboard. Josephine picked it up fast and steered them out the last of the river to open water.

No one fell out of the boat, but it was a long, rough, and bruising ride back in. They took a few waves over the bow, and all three were wet and exhausted by the time they got back to the marina at Key West. The pounding ride hadn't done Sara any good, in spite of her sister sitting on the deck holding her head in her lap most of the way. She was unconscious when Taco Bob laid her on the bed in the guest room of his houseboat.

"What do you say to us getting her on over to the hospital, Josephine?" He was pretty sure what the answer would be, but asked anyway.

"N-no!"

Josephine had looked like she was going to get seasick at first, but pulled through, and even ran the boat once to give him a break on the way back. She'd come through the ordeal determined.

"L-let's c-call Lydia!"

* * *

I spent most of the day in the garden at the hotel, collecting treats for my Josephine. I've noticed that not only am I invisible to most humans, but bugs can't see me either. Makes it easier to sneak up on them.

I just hope Lydia didn't see that plastic bag of flowers and crickets sliding across the floor towards Josephine's room. Not to mention the mango that rolled in the front door and across the lobby.

Chapter 11
Quarantine

The sun made its usual departure, casually making the rounds across the planet like it had for millennia. A strong young wind had shown up earlier and was itching to go. The sun had seen it all before. It wasn't much impressed with show-offs.

"Key West Manor Hotel. Hey, Sis! Did you find her?"

Lydia was not having a good day. The cops were being a pain about letting Consuelo go. Some crap about court and judges or something. She was pretty sure they were just being hard-asses because officer Sanchez had taken a fall. Even Brad's lawyer-friend couldn't talk any sense into them.

Then when she'd gotten back to the hotel, Brad was gone. He was such a conscientious person, she couldn't believe he would just take off like that without at least leaving a note. Maybe some kind of emergency had come up at work.

Not to mention the whole town was going nuts since she'd gotten back from the jail. The weather service had issued a hurricane watch that included Key West, so non-residents were being advised to leave as soon as possible. There were several guests milling around in the lobby, and the rest had either left already or were in their rooms packing.

At least they'd found Sara. But from Josephine's phone report, it sounded like she was in a bad way.

"Josephine, ask Taco Bob to help you with Sara and bring her here to the hotel. They've got an evacuation going on because of the hurricane, so everything is pretty crazy. Be careful."

Brad was coming around. The taser had really kicked his ass, and it had taken him a while to figure out what was going on.

He was lying on the floor of a really small motel bathroom and had an excellent view of the areas that never got cleaned. The place was obviously one of the older motels on the island and long overdue for a remodel. From his vantage point, it looked and smelled like a long war had been fought between pine-oil cleaner and every imaginable filth, with the former in dire need of reinforcements. Despite his hands and feet being wrapped with duct tape, he managed to get into a sitting position. The smell wasn't any better, but the view wasn't quite as bad.

He assumed the muffled voices he heard through the bathroom door were the two men he remembered just before everything went bad.

∽

"Okay, we're looking good here, Louie. I'm gonna go give the boss a call and tell him we got his boy. I gave that André clown enough cash he shouldn't bother us, but if he comes by again saying we gotta leave the motel because of the storm, just tell him to go fuck himself. I'll be right back."

Louie was still wound up from the grab. As soon as Gus went out to use the pay phone, he went to his room next door to freshen up. The palms around the old motel were making a lot of racket from the wind, and that didn't help his nerves any. On the way back from his room, Louie could see that the main road leading out of town was jammed full of cars. It was a little weird the way they got the green light on the grab about the same time the word came down to evac the island. It was time to get Gus to spill what he knew about the job.

∽

"Mr. Dent? Mr. Greenfield will see you now."

Fred Dent, formerly Derek Thurstron, formerly of the CIA, nodded to Greenfield's secretary and went into the big man's office. Like all your better New York offices, it had a spectacular view of Central Park, but the most noticeable thing in the room was the giant map showing MegaDrug's holdings across the world. There were thousands of different-colored lights across the map. Some were blinking.

"Fred, come on in. Have a seat."

Fred took the seat in front of the huge desk. The old man was wired, as usual, pacing in front of the window looking down on the world below. He was running his hand through his perfect gray CEO hair and chewing on an unlit cigar stub. He pointed at one of the blinking lights on the map.

"Got that little problem taken care of in Kansas City this morning, Fred. Got some dirt on one of the nuns. Harold says the contract went through for less than our original offer. Damn smart boy, that Harold."

Fred didn't say anything. He knew the old man would wind down eventually. Always liked to play the people in Acquisitions against each other. Old Greenfield was a brilliant businessman, but he was also an asshole.

"It's people like Harold who are making MegaDrug what it is today, Fred. Harold is one of those rare visionaries who sees that people are not only living longer these days, but they're getting weaker. Most of them sit on their ass all day at work, drive home, and then sit on their ass in front of the television!" Greenfield gestured towards the window. "Whole damn country is full of people falling apart! There's so many things wrong with them, it's easier for the doctors to just prescribe some pills!"

The old man was even more worked up than usual. Fred had often wondered what kind of free experimental drug samples were available to the head of the second largest drugstore chain in the country.

"Harold can see the future, Fred. He can see the day when there will be more drugstores in every town than there are gas stations!"

Fred had heard it all before, but he knew the real score. One, Harold was a no-class Neanderthal who got kicked out of one of the big crime families for his overly brutal nature. Two, an independent contractor working one of Harold's jobs in northern California flipped out completely and old Greenfield woke up in his bed one night with a metallic taste in his mouth. The cold, steel barrel of a .44 would do that, especially while still in the hand of a cracked professional with a message to deliver. The old man was even more nuts since that little incident.

"But enough about Harold, what have you got for me, Fred?"

Fred had been with MegaDrug for a couple years now. Worked his way up to Regional Director of Acquisitions for the Southeast US quickly after losing his job with the CIA in Central America. He'd been a rising star with The Company in Resource Distribution before some of the promising young revolutionaries he'd supplied with automatic weapons decided to try them out on some US missionaries.

"Mr. Greenfield, we're moving on the Key West thing. We have contractors in position and have completed phase one in Operation Get Outta Town."

The old man took a seat behind the desk and seemed to become aware of the unlit cigar in his mouth for the first time. He threw it away and took a fresh one from the humidor on his desk. Fred noticed the little facial twitch the old man had sometimes was starting. He usually got that when he was making plans to fuck somebody. Greenfield smiled severely and gestured for him to continue while he went through his usual cigar-lighting ritual.

"A hurricane watch was issued for the lower Keys a few hours ago, sir. Non-residents are already leaving the island, and if the storm continues its current path, the next step would be a mandatory evacuation order for everyone in the lower Keys and Key West. It's looking very likely this will happen, sir."

Greenfield finished sniffing and licking, and had a gold lighter on the end of his cigar. He puffed away. "Run the whole thing by me, Fred, the big picture."

"Yes sir. It doesn't really matter if the hurricane hits the island or not. Once most of the people are off the island, we fax the report to the Center for Disease Control in Atlanta. A new, even deadlier, strain of West Nile Fever has been discovered to be the cause of several recent deaths in Key West. Since the report will be from the head biologist and director of the Health Department, the authorities will have no choice but to quarantine the island. No one will be allowed back into Key West."

"I like it, Fred. Go on, tell me the rest." He was sure the old man knew the rest, after all, it was mostly his idea. Greenfield never tired of hearing about one of his sleazy plans working. The cigar lighter went back on the desk. It looked like a giant gold pill.

"Certainly, sir. Key West is one of the tightest real-estate markets in the country. If we can keep the island quarantined for a few days, there should be a significant decline in property values. Most of the businesses there are running such a close overhead that a few days without cash flow will put them under.

"Business owners will panic. Our advance strike force from Purchasing is standing by to move in on your orders, sir. They'll field-coordinate the deployment of the other teams while Legal and Financial do the follow-ups from here. We'll have some serious deals already in the oven before anyone else even comes in. It should take a few weeks for the CDC to be sure there isn't any fever outbreak. By then MegaDrug will be a major player in Key West real estate, just in time for prices to go right back up."

The old man was following every word, puffing and twitching away. Fred knew dear Harold would be getting an earful soon. This was a big move for MegaDrug, they were pulling out all the stops to raise capital for their continuing push to build more drugstores. If they pulled this off, they might even pass Jack's Drugs as #1 in the world.

"I've been working with Diane in Accounting, sir. I'm sure she can give you some more solid numbers, but it looks like the turnaround should be around six months and net an easy two hundred to three hundred million.

"The only possible problem would be if the health department official turns up to deny sending the fax to Atlanta, which is highly unlikely, since he's the guest of our contractors as we speak."

By the time Jeremy made it back to the hotel it was getting dark. As he was riding the bike through the windy streets, he'd been thinking about the new girls at the strip club. Thinking about them had been better than thinking about what Lydia was going to say to him about being gone all day.

Several hours of drinking and ogling hadn't helped his equilibrium any, and he crash-landed the bicycle into the side of the hotel's garage.

"Jeremy!"

Jeremy's relief at finding himself unhurt from the fall was tempered by the look on Lydia's face. He ducked the flashlight she threw at him.

"All the shutters on the hotel are fully secured before you come inside!"

Jeremy started to protest but held when Lydia took a step toward him.

"Otherwise you're riding out the storm hanging from that flagpole!"

Jeremy knew where the flagpole was, but he looked anyway. The wind made the cable clang against the pole. Jeremy abandoned the bicycle and scurried off for a ladder.

"That was just Jeremy. He's going to close the shutters on the windows."

Lydia was back inside with Josephine at Sara's bedside. Sara was still out, and Josephine was putting up an IV bag to get more fluids into her patient.

"Th-the trip b-back in d-didn't do her m-much good. It was p-pretty rough."

"She looks so different. I never would have recognized her."

"I'll g-get her b-better, don't worry."

Josephine gave her sister a smile that was supposed to be reassuring, and it worked. Lydia could see her little sister had things under control with Sara, she was taking charge of the situation, something she had rarely done in the past. Lydia was glad for the help, since there were plenty of other things she needed to be dealing with.

The Hurricane Watch had been upgraded to a Warning, with a forty percent chance of it hitting Key West with winds of 135 miles per hour. This little bit of news had most of the hard-core partiers, and even locals who had been through storms in the past, heading for the exits. Or exit, in this case, since there was only one road in or out of the Keys.

US 1 was bumper-to-bumper. Cars that hadn't been out of Key West in years joined the exodus. Keys Cruisers with hand painted scenes on their rusting bodies were leaving packed full of exotic pets and record collections. Those who hadn't already left were doing what they could to secure their property before heading for the mainland.

The last of the guests from the hotel were long gone, and Lydia was on the phone with the police department at the front desk. Someone there told her Consuelo should be released on her own recognizance because of the storm, so she was on hold while they tried to find out when. The wind was making a lot of noise outside and she was reaching for the remote to turn up the sound on the television when the front door burst open.

"Howdy, Pa! I'm home from the wars!"

Consuelo, swaggered in like a B-movie gunslinger. Lydia slammed down the phone.

"Consuelo!"

She ran over and gave her sister a big hug. Plenty of smiles.

"They ain't made a jail yet could hold me!" Consuelo was still hamming it up. "So what's up, Sis? Sure hope we got plenty of beer, doing time makes me powerful thirsty!"

Lydia was so glad to see Consuelo. She grabbed her by the hand and started walking toward the back of the hotel.

"What's up, you ask? Well, let's see. All the guests have left the hotel. There's a category four hurricane on the way." They heard a blood-curdling scream and a crash outside. "Jeremy's out there closing the storm shutters. And Sara is here." Lydia pulled her sister through the bedroom doorway.

"Sara!"

Consuelo stared at her emaciated sister sleeping on the bed. The usually perky blond looked with tears in her eyes at her other two sisters.

There was a small voice from the bed. "Hey, Sis." Sara's eyes came open and she managed a weak smile. "What do you have to do to get a drink around here?"

* * *

Josephine spent the night by her sister's bed. After Sara went back to sleep, her other sisters left and I came down out of the vents and kept my lover company. She really does know a lot about taking care of people when they're sick.

One of her teachers showed her things about using plants in medicines and even tried to teach her how to talk to plants. The teacher told her it makes it a lot easier when you can ask a plant directly if it's good for healing. Josephine said she hasn't quite got the hang of that yet. She told me talking to plants sounds a little crazy.

Chapter 12

Hurricane Warnings

*The wind came in like an obnoxious drunk
at his own party. It got loud, told off-color
jokes to those who didn't want to hear them,
and pinched the pretty sky on the ass. By the
time the rain clouds showed up, everyone else
was leaving.*

"So what's it going to do?"

Early the next morning Consuelo was drinking coffee with Lydia at the front desk and watching the Weather Channel. They had decided to stay put and ride out the storm. They didn't want to move Sara again, and the old hotel had been through hurricanes before.

"Sounds like the weather geeks don't even know. Been just sitting there for the last few hours."

The storm had stalled during the night. It was still very windy in Key West, with the occasional rain squall from the big storm's outside feeder bands. None of the few people remaining on the island had had a very good night. The police had come by after dark and tried to get the sisters to evacuate, but Consuelo used her natural charm and recent reputation as an assaulter of police officers to convince them to move on.

Lydia poured herself another coffee and switched to one of the news channels. A reporter was standing on a windy beach somewhere in the Keys getting soaked from the rain and salt spray off the huge waves. He looked miserable.

"That's right, Brian. If the people of Key West didn't have enough problems already with a major hurricane threatening, now there's a quarantine order in effect for the entire island. We've just learned that the Centers for Disease Control in Atlanta has asked local law enforcement not to allow anyone on or off the island until reports can be confirmed concerning an outbreak of a new, possibly deadlier, strain of West Nile Virus. This reporter suspects this new strain will be called the Key West Nile Virus."

The soaked man on the beach looked proud of that, then almost went down from a wind gust before continuing.

"According to the statement released earlier by the CDC, several recent deaths on the island may be attributed to the virus. While interviewing several of the storm evacuees earlier today, this reporter was told there were a number of dead birds found in the beach area. As you know Brian, a high mortality rate in birds is often the result of mosquito-borne viruses like West Nile. I'll have more after this quick break."

Lydia and Consuelo sat glued to the television through eight long minutes of commercials and promos. Lydia confirmed the bird thing to her sister who had switched from coffee to beer. The station finally went back to the reporter after the news anchor did an intro. The reporter was having a hard time standing his ground in the wind and his microphone was starting to cut out.

"That's r ... Brian, the CDC has said that ... to contact the biologist from the Key West Health Department who filed the report just yesterday, the total quarantine of the island of Key W ... remain in effect. The Key West Police Department has so far been unable to reach Dr. Brad Mulberry, and has ... on speculation that he may have evacuated with the majority of the islands residents."

The reporter had caught a few waves on the ankles during his report, but the one that got him behind the knees was a complete surprise. He went down and the waves started pulling him out to sea. A bald man wearing headphones and carrying a clipboard ran into the surf after the reporter just as the station cut to Sports.

"Hey! They're talking about Brad! Brad's a biologist, and he works for the city! Holy shit, Consuelo!" Lydia was on her feet and pacing the lobby. Consuelo didn't pay much attention to her sister, she was staring at the television.

"How much do you think those reporters make?"

Josephine was feeling pretty good. She hadn't gotten much sleep in the chair next to Sara's bed during the night, but seeing her patient awake and looking better in the morning made her forget about the lack of sleep.

"M-more soup?"

Sara was sitting up in bed and finishing off her second bowl of the morning. Her other sisters had been in to see her, and Lydia told them about their neighbor Brad and the quarantine.

"Maybe a little more later on. I could get used to this treatment, you know." Sara gave her little sister a smile.

They had a lot of catching up to do and had been at it while Consuelo monitored the television in the lobby and kept an eye on Lydia going across the street to Brad's house. Sara was telling the story of her former lover and guru Charlie Spider.

"When I came here I was convinced I could bring him back, and I thought I had, for a while at least."

From what her sister was saying, it sounded to Josephine like Sara had been trying to bring some old guy back from the dead. She remembered what Taco Bob had said about Sara having some odd ideas.

"I thought if I could get him out to the little cabin in the swamp we would be happy, just the two of us. I don't remember much of what happened after I left Key West though, I must have started getting the fever not long after I got back to the cabin. I spent days at a time in fever dreams, lost in strange worlds, looking for Charlie."

Sara shrugged and gave her sister a little smile. "Men. Make you do the craziest things sometimes."

She winked and Josephine reached over and gave her hand a little squeeze. She wondered if she should mention her own affair with an eight-inch alien who no one except her could see but decided there was something more important first.

"S-sara. I n-need to t-tell you about m-mom."

When Lydia went across the street to Brad's house the wind still howled, but the rain had let up. Before she got back to the hotel, it started pouring again and she was soaked. She was drying her hair with a towel when she came back to the front desk. Consuelo was doing sit-ups and watching the television.

"I don't like it, Sis. The place was unlocked, like usual, but there were windows open and the wind and rain were making a mess inside the house. His motorcycle is in the garage, so if he left it was with someone else. I've just got a bad feeling about it." She looked at the television. "Any news on the storm?"

∞

Two figures trudged slowly through the deserted streets of Key West. They leaned into the wind and rain holding hands to help keep their balance. One had a firm grip on a hat and the other a shawl as they negotiated their way toward the hotel.

∞

It took a while, but Josephine finally got it all out about their mother dying over a year ago and their selling the Majestic and moving to Key West. She told Sara about their mother's last wish that the three sisters should find their long-lost older sister. Sara listened carefully and seemed to take the news about their mother fairly well. Then it was her turn.

"I'm really sorry to hear about Rosa dying, Josephine, she was a kind and gentle person. From what you've told me, I think I know why she wanted you to find me."

∞

A particularly strong gust of wind nearly caused one of the figures to lose his footing as they came around a corner.

His orange cape was flapping furiously as they neared the front door of the hotel.

✧

"Well, at least we haven't lost electricity or the phone yet. If that storm starts this way again it's liable to be a long, dark night."

Consuelo was listening to her sister while she ran in place by the front desk and kept an eye on the television. She really wanted to go out for a run, but Lydia was adamant. Lydia was also wired, pacing back and forth in the lobby. Her pale hands dancing in the air as she talked.

"I'm going to see how Josey and Sara are doing while you're working out. Maybe see if I can get Jeremy out of bed." Just as she started for the back, Josephine came in with a blank look on her face. "What is it Josey? You look like you've seen a ghost."

Josephine slowly walked to one of the couches and sat. Immediately both her sisters sat across from her.

"We n-n-need to talk."

The front door banged open and Orange Dali and Ms Doris staggered into the lobby dripping water. Lydia and Consuelo jumped to their feet and stared in disbelief as the woman took off her shawl. They glanced at each other, then said in unison, "Wiola!"

Josephine looked even paler than before. She slowly raised her hand and pointed at their teacher who was smiling mischievously and taking a small bow.

"T-that's our r-real m-mother!"

* * *

Josephine and her sisters were pretty worked
up over that. It looked like a good story coming
up, so I got comfortable in the air vent above
the front desk. I was thinking some munchies
would be nice. Then I remembered the stray
cheetos I'd found under the sofa cushions. You
can't get snacks like that where I come from.

Chapter 13

Mother

Gusts of wind and stinging rain came
through the islands like visiting in-laws'
spoiled children on too much sugar.

"Hurricane Zenobia is still stationary and packing winds in excess of 130 miles per hour as of the last reporting period. Air Force reconnaissance planes are expected to have an update on the storm within the next hour. At this time the Cuban government has not released information on casualities or the extent of damage from the hurricane, how-ever two men from a local news camera crew are reported missing in the Florida Keys. In sports —"

Louie killed the sound on the television and stretched back in the only chair in the room.

"I gotta hand it to you Gus, my man, the thing with throwing rat poison to the birds on the beach was a stroke of genius."

Gustov was propped up on the tiny motel room's bed with a big smile and a bag of chips. He wasn't about to tell his partner it was a strange twist of luck with the birds or that the same stuff worked on abusive alcoholic fathers. He really hadn't even thought about the tie-in with the job, he just liked poisoning seagulls.

"Yeah, the boss says our client is pretty happy with the way things are going. I just hope this fucking hurricane doesn't actually come through here. A big storm surge flooding the whole island and drowning everyone might complicate things." Since he had finally been briefed on the whole scam, Louie was feeling pretty good about the way the job was going himself. At least he had been until the mention of the storm surge thing.

"Whadaya talking about here? I thought that was why you picked this crummy motel in the first place? Didn't you say it was one of the higher places on this rock? Plus we're on the third floor! Don't be giving me any of your shit here, Gus!"

Hard looks were something the big man had learned in prison. He gave his partner one.

"Just be glad we haven't lost cable, my little friend. I get real crazy if I don't have cable."

He reached down under the bed for another bag of corn chips. There was a week's worth of supplies under the bed. Louie wasn't too sure about spending several more days in the cramped little room with the man. At least he had his own room next door for getting some sleep, and unlike his partner's room, it didn't have a biologist tied up in the bathroom.

Brad was sore from lying on the hard tile floor. Like everyone else on the island, he'd had a rough night, but for a different reason. He managed to cut the duct tape holding his hands behind him on a sharp edge of the shower doors. Not all the way through, just got it started so these guys wouldn't know what he was up to.

He'd gotten the hang of turning on the sink faucet with his nose so he could get a drink around the gag tied in his mouth. They'd taken his pants and underwear off him so he could relieve himself at least. It wasn't easy to do with your hands and feet tied, but it beat the alternative.

∞

At the Key West Manor Hotel, there didn't seem to be any shortage of things to talk about. After the initial period of stunned silence, the three sisters started talking at once. Still smiling, Wiola held up a hand for silence.

"Josephine is right, or course. You must have spoken with Sara."

Lydia took a step forward.

"She's here. Josephine found her in the swamps on the mainland."

Wiola raised an eyebrow and gave the youngest of her daughters an approving nod. Lydia looked bewildered, a new look for her.

"Is it true, Wiola, that you're our real mother? Then what about Rosa?"

Orange Dali, overly shy at the best of times, eased unnoticed toward a chair by the wall. Consuelo noticed.

"Hey, let's all sit down, maybe you can explain what's going on."

The sisters all had healthy amounts of respect and fear for their teacher. They carefully arranged themselves on the lobby couches around Wiola, while Orange Dali did his best to look inconspicuous sitting against the wall hiding under his big floppy hat. A branch whipping in the wind started banging against the back of the hotel.

"You said Sara is here? Is she well?"

Lydia took it.

"She's only been here since yesterday. She had a fever when she was in the swamp, but she's on the mend, just really weak still. Josephine has been taking care of her." Josephine got another eyebrow from her long-time teacher.

"I see, so all four of you are together then." The older woman seemed to be considering this before continuing. "It's a bit of a long story, you know. I am your mother, each of you came from this womb."

Wiola pressed both hands to her abdomen. For a woman of fifty who'd given birth to four daughters, she was in remarkable shape. And obviously knew it. She glanced at the young artist. So did the sisters.

"I came to Key West just a few days after you moved here. I have a little house on the other side of Duval. Mr. Dali here is a friend; he stays with me sometimes." She waited to see if this would draw a comment.

"But how can you be our mother? Rosa was our mother!"

Lydia wanted to know what was going on, now, and the look in her eyes made this very apparent. Wiola had vanished without a word about the same time Rosa had died. There was so much tension in the room Orange Dali's knees were beginning to shake. Wiola made a dismissive motion with her hand and continued.

"You see, my dears, I was not always the model of impeccable style and grace you see here before you today." She gave her soaked and disheveled hair a little push with the palm of her hand. "I had a bit of a bad period. For several years I was quite mad, you know."

There didn't seem to be anyone in the room who was going to question this.

"Other than I never knew who my parents were, I was a fairly normal child by rural Mississippi standards. I was raised, along with several other orphans, by dirt-poor foster parents. I knew poverty and hard times, and my future was bleak. But I was fortunate to meet, and eventually marry, a very wonderful, and very rich, man. We were quite happy together and were blessed with a healthy, though painfully ordinary, daughter.

"My husband's work with the family business required him to travel occasionally, and he always took Sara and me along with him. One time in Mexico, the three of us were walking to a river for a picnic outside of the town where we were staying. It was a beautiful day when we left the hotel, but a storm came up suddenly and there was tremendous lighting and thunder. Not many people lived in the area, and we were fortunate to see a large hacienda not far away.

"The lightning was intense, so we started to run toward the house. I stopped to pick up little Sara just as a huge lightning bolt hit my poor husband in the top of the head." Wiola pointed a finger at the crown of her head. "Killed him instantly, of course, and nearly killed Sara and myself, we were so close.

"When I came to several days later I was in the hacienda. There was a man there, an American, and several others of different nationalities, but mostly Mexicans and

Indians. I had no memory of what had happened, so when they told me my husband was dead, I nearly lost my mind. They said that while I had been unconscious his relatives had been notified and had already taken the body back to the states. Since the relatives had never approved of our marriage, it was convenient for them to leave a woman and child, neither of whom would probably ever fully recover, to fend for themselves.

"But we did recover, mostly. Sara healed faster than I, and the people who lived in the hacienda had one of their maids, a woman named Rosa, take care of her. Besides my poor physical condition from the lightning strike, I was nearly overwhelmed with grief from losing my wonderful husband. The American man saw that I had lost my will to live as well as my sanity, so he tricked me into getting better.

"He told me that Rosa was really a sorceress who was going to do all kinds of terrible things to my little girl. I was horrified at the thought of someone hurting this poor child who had already gone through so much. I was a superstitious and ignorant woman in those days who was frightened spitless at the thought of witches or sorcerers."

Everyone in the room looked at once at the short bald man standing in the doorway. He had just walked up and was listening while eating half a cheeto he'd found on the front desk. He stopped chewing when he saw the women looking at him.

"Uh, I think I'll go around back and see what's banging against the building." And was gone.

"Anyway," Wiola said, "the American convinced me that the only way I could save my daughter from the evil witch Rosa was to learn sorcery from the other people living there who, as it conveniently turned out, were also sorcerers."

Wiola smiled at her three daughters who were hanging on every word.

"But the trick worked. With the man's encouragement, I became obsessed with learning sorcery from the people in that house and started recovering. Of course, it turned out that Rosa was the only one there who wasn't a sorcerer. But by the time I figured that out, I didn't care. I spent four years with those people and discovered worlds I never in my wildest dreams knew existed. Sara had become close to Rosa, so when the man from the hacienda took us with him back to the states, she came along as nanny." Wiola paused, she seemed to know it was coming. Lydia spoke up.

"Rosa told us our father had died soon after Josephine was born."

"Ah yes, probably the only lie that dear soul ever told. She did love you girls, and she was a much better mother to you than I would have ever been." The older woman sighed, then smiled before she went on.

"The American was a seeker who had come to that house only a few days earlier looking for a sign from spirit. He was looking out the window when he got his sign: a lightning bolt hit three people running toward the house he was in.

"He took it as his task to help us. After we came back to the US with him, Rosa and Sara stayed in California while we traveled the world together. After a few years, and three children, he traveled more by himself. His name was Logan, and yes my dears, he was not only your other teacher for years, but he is also your father."

The banging coming from the back of the hotel stopped, followed by a muffled yell. The only sound was the wind and rain trying to get inside the old hotel.

"Before he left for the Orient a few weeks ago, he suggested I come here to enjoy the change of air and to make sure you girls were all right. You see, we may not be the most normal of parents, but we do love you and worry about you."

The wind outside kept at it, but it was eerily quiet in the old hotel lobby. Wiola clapped her hands together and brought her daughters out of their thoughts and back into the room.

"I almost forgot! The reason we came by is because dear Dali saw two suspicious men carry someone out of your hotel yesterday. He was so upset about it the poor dear couldn't bring himself to talk about it until this morning. Are you missing anyone?"

* * *

Jeremy is like a walking bruise these days. Man has enough trouble with ladders and heights without trying to get a limb away from the hotel during a storm. I even kind of felt sorry for him, watching out the window as he blew off the ladder with the limb in his hand.

Then I saw him pull a bucket out of the bushes and stand on it peeking in one of the windows. The window to the bathroom Josephine shares with her sisters. My feelings of pity turned into thoughts of plots.

Chapter 14

Brad

The wind and rain behaved like a couple of teenagers arguing over a pinball machine. Neither one was right, but neither would admit to being wrong. It was a boring argument that had been heard a thousand times, but the wind and rain argued on just for the sake of arguing.

"I gotta take a dump. Let me have the key to your room."

That was the only thing about this job Louie was having a problem with now. Gustov using his bathroom. Man was an animal. A big smelly animal.

"Guess I'll check in with the boss down at the pay phone while I'm at it."

Louie made a big production of handing over the key. He had an extra one he could give the big man, but he liked making him ask for it. Louie picked imaginary lint off his jacket and changed the channel on the television. His partner was one of those people who could watch the Weather Channel for hours at a time. It was driving him nuts.

"Hey, you think you could at least flush the toilet over there this time?" Gustov gave him a snort as he headed out the door.

Louie started watching some crazy shit on the Food Channel about cooking eels. He had the sound turned down and was listening over the wind for Gustov to slam the door when he finished abusing his bathroom. When he heard the door, he peeked out the curtain and saw his partner heading down the stairs towards the phone. Time for a quick freshening-up himself that Gustov didn't need to know about.

Brad's heart was pounding in his throat. He'd still been a little out of it when they put him in the bathroom, so he didn't know if these guys were armed with anything other than the stun gun. He had no clue why they'd kidnapped him. They must have thought he was someone else.

He couldn't hear what was being said through the bathroom door, but he knew one of them, then the other, had left. It was his chance. After furiously cutting the tape the rest of the way through on the edge of the shower door, Brad got his feet free, the gag out of his mouth, and his pants on. He was a little wobbly after being tied up for so long, but the adrenaline was getting him carefully out the bathroom door, four steps to the room door, and then running through the wind for the stairs.

Louie still had the bathroom vent fan going trying to get rid of Gustov's residual odors while he was soaping-up his hands and wasn't sure. Was that the wind, or did he hear the door to the other room?

Joey Two Thumbs sounded a little lit. He was going on about how pleased his client, MegaDrug, was with the way things were going so far. Gustov figured this was a little unusual. Joey must be in an extra good mood to be hitting the sauce so early and talking about a client by name, two things he rarely did. A few raindrops found Gustov and he looked up at the stormy afternoon sky. The clouds were really moving. He noticed it was getting darker when he saw something in the deserted motel parking lot that made his heart skip a beat.

"Yeah, look Joey, we might have a little problem here. I gotta go." The ass-chewing he was sure to get for hanging up on his boss was the least of his worries at the moment.

Brad had had plenty of time to plan his escape, but hadn't thought past getting out of the room. He figured the roads would be packed with cars leaving the island, but the streets were deserted. When he got to the other side of the parking lot he did a quick turn around to get his bearings. He wasn't that far from the police station, figured he'd run in that direction and hopefully get a ride. Someone had to come along.

Must have been the wind blowing something against the building. Louie was glad to see his partner hadn't come back to the room yet. Maybe he was getting some ice from the machine. Maybe he was shooting the shit with the boss still. Whatever.

Probably ought to check on the guy in the can. Seemed to be sleeping every time they looked in there. Most likely faking it, but hey, makes it easier on everyone that way. Check on him the next commercial. These Jap guys were still cooking the fucking eels. Some people will eat anything.

Gustov thought his heart was going to explode. The run to the car and the panic he was dealing with was just about too much. He needed to start going to the gym, maybe lose a few pounds.

Up ahead. Guy was running, stopped, and put out his thumb like he was hitchhiking. Nobody else on the road. Wind and raining hard enough the guy can't see inside the car. Slow a little, drive past. Turn around and go back to the guy. Get up close like you're going to roll down the window, ask him what's up. Slow, but don't stop. Open the door instead, catch the guy in the knees, he's down. Jump out. Guy's all flopping around, not cooperative. A foot to the back of the neck, then tape him up again and put him in the trunk. Nice size trunk. Always pays to get the full-size rental in this line of work.

Louie couldn't believe these people were eating this eel shit. They seemed to really get off on it. Give him a steak and potatoes any day. Gus is back suddenly, all wet.

"You fuck!"

Gustov slammed the door and went for his partner's throat. Louie fell back in his chair and started kicking the big man as hard as he could.

"Get the fuck off me! The fuck is wrong with you!"

Louie got his gun out and started hitting the big man in the side of the head with it. After a few whacks the pressure around his neck started easing up. Gustov let go and fell back on the bed holding the side of his head with one hand and going for his own gun with the other.

"Go ahead, Louie! Take a look in the bathroom!"

Both men had guns pointed at the other. Louie didn't want to look in the bathroom. He was in deep shit. He looked in the bathroom.

"How the fuck —"

"You went next door to screw around instead of staying here while I was gone, didn't you?"

There was murder in Gustov's eyes. Louie could only think about those little eel-eating Jap fucks. Somehow this was their fault.

"I ought to just whack your sorry ass and throw you to the crabs! When I tell the boss you almost let him get away, he'll probably wet you himself."

The frantic thoughts flying around inside Louie's head grabbed onto one thing.

"You said almost? You got him?"

The fire died down a notch in the big man's eyes.

"Yeah, I saved your skinny ass. Boss told me earlier we might want to get rid of him when this is over. Maybe you should do it now, by yourself, since you got your gun handy. Think you could cap a man tied up in the trunk of a car without fucking it up?"

The gun in Louie's hand had been slowly coming down, but this insult brought it back up. The two men locked eyes and pointed guns. The only sound was the wind and rain outside and some Japanese guys laughing their asses off on the television. Gustov's gun hand tightened and Louie slowly brought his other hand up for a better grip.

There was a knock at the door. The two men looked at the door and then at each other.

"Who is it?"

A female voice.

"Housekeeping!"

* * *

First thing I did was drag Jeremy's bucket over a few feet in the bushes under a big wasp nest. He'll probably think the wind blew it. Next time he wants to use his bucket to get an eyeful, he will.

Chapter 15
Guests

The wind droned on like a college professor up for tenure. The clouds sat in the front row and hung on every word like a fifth-year student needing a passing grade to get a degree in meteorology. The rain was bored to tears and wanted to sneak out for a smoke; it had its sights set on a career in shutting down sporting events.

"Housekeeping?"

Louie was pretty sure everyone was gone from the hotel except the clown André up front in the office. Guy was always there. Joey Thumbs was the only other person who knew they were in the room, and a personal visit from Joey was never good news.

"Louie, see who the fuck that is!"

Louie kept his eyes on his partner as he put his gun back in the shoulder holster under his linen coat. He stood and straightened his clothes while Gustov slipped his gun under the bed pillow. The big man on the bed motioned toward the door. Louie opened the door just a crack.

"You gotta take theese towels, ees motel rules! Clean towels everday!"

There was a fine set of knockers just under the voice. Not big, but nicely displayed knockers, barely restrained by a maid's uniform trying to flap open in the wind. Louie opened the door a little more for a better look. The owner of the knockers pushed a maid's cart against the door and Louie stepped back.

"Here, you take theese towels, meester!"

As the cart came into the room a stack of towels was shoved roughly into his chest and the maid's hands touched his jacket. As soon as the cart was through the door a little blond came out of it and went like a crab on all fours towards the man on the bed. Before Gus could get his hand from under the pillow she was on him. Two strong hands grabbed his wrist and he got a solid head-butt.

"Get on the floor!"

The maid had Louie's gun pointed inches from his face, and the blond was on her feet with the other gun. The big man looked dazed and out of it on the bed.

"The fuck is going on here?"

Louie was still holding the towels.

"Face-down, on the floor! Now!"

The maid looked so wired he was afraid she might start shooting. Blondie motioned with her gun for him to go down. He did.

"Check the bathroom, Lyd."

When the maid came back out of the bathroom, she didn't look like she'd found what she was looking for.

"He's not in there!"

Gustov was moaning on the bed and sat up holding his forehead. The blond stuck the man's own gun in his face.

"Where is he? Where's Brad?"

The big man came out of it enough to groan an answer.

"I don't know what you're talking about."

The two women looked at each other and shrugged. The maid took a step toward the door and spoke loud enough for the lookout outside to hear.

"Guess we'll have to bring in the negotiator!"

A small, dark-haired beauty slipped into the room and closed the door. She was smiling in a very unsettling way. There were a lot of nice things to look at on this one, but Louie couldn't stop staring at her eyes. They were as black and shiny as polished obsidian.

Stevie Nine-Fingers was not a happy man. His vacation in paradise had been for shit so far. He no sooner hit town than there's some storm coming, evacuation order for all the tourists. Stevie figured maybe this could be a good situation; bars were too crowded anyway, thin things out a little. Maybe hook-up with some local hottie, do some serious partying.

Then he found out the bars all had to close. No liquor sales when there's an evac for the island. So much for hurricane parties.

But he got himself in a situation anyway involving this chubby dancer from the strip club, a family-size bottle of good scotch, and this tiny-ass motel room. It wasn't exactly a scene from "Casablanca", but he did have a hangover worthy of an Oscar as he staggered out into the parking lot of the motel. Bimbo was busy heaving her guts out in the bathroom, so he'd decided to get some air. He was thinking the air back home in New Jersey would be about right.

He hated Chevys; but it was the only car in the lot, so he found the right master key and got in. Weather was sure fucked in this town. Blowing like a bitch with occasional stinging rain was not what he had in mind when he'd decided to take some time off from his job with the chop shop.

He was in supply. Turned professional when he found out he could make a helluva lot more money in vehicular provision than working for his uncle the locksmith.

Bad was the situation with the law, which had him leaving town once in a while when things got a little hot. Good was you pretty much set your own hours, and with his locksmith experience, he didn't have to jack around with slim-jims and hammer drills. He had the key thing down.

Current situation called for dealing with the local yokels and this quarantine bullshit. Seen it on the news they weren't letting anyone on or off the island. What the fuck was going on? Stevie didn't know better, he'd think someone had it in for him.

Cruise the bridge leading off the island. Not much of a bridge, pretty short. Nothing compared to some of the ones he'd seen a couple days earlier driving that little convertible down the Keys. Some bullshit barricade up across the bridge and a couple cops talking to some people. Hard-core locals didn't want to leave when the evac came down. Start with the quarantine, and suddenly everybody wants to leave. A few people looking pretty pissed off, talking to the cops there in the rain.

Other side of the bridge he could see more police, and TV camera crews, standing around in the crappy weather. Had to get across that bridge.

Air conditioning didn't work in the piece-of-shit Chevy. Figures. Stevie had a plan though, a plan for every situation. Drive down the tourist street there, Duval Street, throw some hunks of rock through a few windows. Nobody around. Couple alarms go off. Anymore cops around, that would give them something to do. Head over to the shopping center he seen coming into town. Thought he might have to use another rock, but found the right key for a side door to Sears. Check out the toy section. Fifteen minutes later he's back at the bridge. Park next to a van by a boat ramp going down into the water. No boats out today, just people arguing with the cops guarding the bridge. Got the carseat in the back and the doll's hand up against the car window. Make sure the windows are up tight, drop the Chevy in gear and run for the cops. Chevy deserved it for not having a/c.

"Hey, officer! I got a bad situation here!" Stevie was looking freaked and pointing at the car going into the water. "My little girl is in that car!"

Every eye goes to the car bobbing along in the waves from the storm. You just could see a small hand inside the car. People screaming and running to get a better look at the car, which was moving down-current fast, away from the bridge.

Stevie could see the cops and cameras on the other side of the bridge all watching the car as it came toward a small mangrove island in the channel. The current pulled the car out of sight behind some trees just as he reached the other side of the bridge. Cops on that side were screaming into

hand-held radios and reporters were screaming at camera-
men.

As afternoon became evening, Stevie Nine Fingers
leisurely cruised across the Seven Mile Bridge looking out
over the white-capped waters in a reporter's Toyota with ice-
cold air conditioning.

Orange Dali had been able to overcome his shyness
when it was made clear to him by the women at the
hotel how important it was. He told them about the men
taking another man out of the hotel. The man looked
sick.

"The man they put in the car, I think he lives around
here. I followed them on a friend's bicycle. They went to
a motel on the other side of the island and I saw them
take the man upstairs. They were acting like the man was
just drunk, but he wasn't. Something was wrong with
him."

He told them the name of the motel, and a plan was laid
out. When they got there, the guy at the front desk got cooperative when the right amount of money was shown. Bor-
row a maid's uniform and cart, and they were in.

"There's some torn duct tape and a pair of underwear in
the bathroom, Consuelo. Briefs."

Louie and Gus were both boxer men, but the most
noticeable element of their current attire was the wraps of
telephone cable.

"Brad wore briefs." The one in the maid's outfit, Lydia,
got a look from the blonde. "Okay, so I didn't come upon

this bit of knowledge the way I would have liked. I helped with his laundry once."

The two men had overcome the initial surprise of the sister's visit and were not happy.

"You little broads better come to your senses and untie us here. You don't know who you're messing with."

Louie had been making threats while the babe with the long dark hair was winding cable around them. Gustov was recovered from the head-butt and pissed. The other two women ignored them after they were tied. They put the guns on the laundry cart and started checking out everything in the room. The dark-haired one with the weird eyes just stood there staring at them. It was creeping them out bad, especially Louie. He was pretty sure she was the same hot number he'd seen around the hotel before. He didn't like the way things were going at all.

"The fuck is her problem? Why's she staring at us like that?"

The blonde called Consuelo was pulling everything out from under the bed. "Lot of supplies here. Enough for a long stay." She stopped for a minute and looked at Louie strapped into the room's lone chair. "You bozos don't want to find out about my sister's little trick with her eyes, you better tell us where Brad is."

While the two men came up with another round of heartfelt, though not all that original, insults and threats, Lydia finished looking over the contents of their wallets.

"These guys are both from Miami. Somebody sent you here to kidnap Brad? This has something to do with the quarantine doesn't it?" Both men got quiet after a few more obscenities. "Last chance to be helpful and still have some of your sanity left for your golden years, boys."

Gus let loose with more of the same, but Louie surprised even himself with the utter vulgarity of his threats. Lydia just looked at them and sighed.

"Thank you, gentlemen, for making this easier for me to say." She motioned to the dark-haired one. "They're all yours, my dear."

Consuelo rolled the big man over so he could see what was going on with his partner, then held Louie's head in an iron grip. Louie started sweating like Niagara Falls.

Brad was wondering what was going on. He was a little thirsty, but the two inches of seawater he was laying in was not what he had in mind.

There was no way they could get a helicopter in the air in that kind of weather, so the police had a boat brought in. Before long there was a good crowd at each end of the bridge braving the weather for a look.

The news people were ecstatic. They had a clip of the sinking car with the baby in back going around a bend in the channel. It was only a few seconds long, so they played it a lot. Plenty of interviews. Officer Muldoon had recently joined the Monroe County Sheriff's Department Motorcycle Division after leaving a similar position on the mainland.

"The Sheriff's Department has assets in place and will be fully investigating this incident in a timely manner." The officer seemed to be happy with what he'd said and was gesturing to a big powerboat on a trailer parked nearby.

"Officer Muldoon, so why aren't they using this boat to find the car with the child in it?" The officer was hoping the reporter wouldn't ask that. He'd been doing so well, too.

"This is a very difficult situation, miss. High winds, rip tides, dangerous currents, those sorts of things. But don't worry, we have everything under control."

The real problem was the only boat ramp for three miles was on the Key West side of the bridge, the quarantine side. Someone finally made a decision, and the boat was driven across the bridge and launched just before dark. Around a corner in the channel the Chevy was perched on a sandbar in a foot of water. The boat was able to get close enough in the rough seas and wind to see there wasn't anything in the car except a plastic doll in a carseat. It was looking like an embarrassing report back on land when they heard yelling from a tiny mangrove island nearby.

"Help! Over here! Somebody help!"

It was another hour after they got back to the boat ramp before someone else finally made a decision and the police boat was allowed back across the bridge to the ever growing crowd of curious public and impatient media. The miraculous rescue of two men from the news team feared lost the day before was the top story on the evening news statewide. Everyone forgot about the Chevy.

Consuelo didn't have to hold Louie's head for very long. After the first few seconds, he was so far gone into Josephine's eyes he was a veg. Lydia was next door checking out Louie's room with the key she'd found in his pocket. Gustov watched from the bed as his partner's face contorted into a silent scream.

"You little bitches fucking better muhmmm ..."

Consuelo slapped a good-size piece of duct tape over Gustov's mouth.

"That will be quite enough of that, Mr. Potty Mouth. You're going to throw off her concentration. But not to worry," she patted him on the arm and winked, "you're next!"

The big man struggled on the bed against the cable for a few minutes before he finally tired. He looked and probably felt like a big helpless slug.

Consuelo came out of the bathroom with a plastic cup of water. Josephine had her face about a foot away from Louie's, giving him the full effect. The well-dressed hood from Miami was still locked in a silent scream.

"Better ease off there, Josey, don't want to give him too much at once and have him blow a tube on us." She gently touched her sister's shoulder. "Blink, Sis."

Josephine did a slow blink and came back away from Louie. Louie slammed his eyes shut, and Lydia could hear him scream from next door. Consuelo tossed the water in his face and he brought it down to a steady sob.

"Maybe took him a bit far, Josey."

Josephine shrugged, and Consuelo got close to whisper in the man's ear. "If you don't want to see the bad little witch's eyes again, I would suggest you tell us where Brad is."

Once Louie was able to speak again, he told everything he knew. He definitely didn't want to go back inside those eyes. Just to be on the safe side, he kept his eyes closed until he was untied and allowed to go into the bathroom to relieve his aching bowels. An hour later, they had the same story on Brad from the big man after he took a look down inside the pit behind those black eyes. Besides ratting out their boss and the client, the big tough guy also peed his pants.

෴

Lydia had already looked for the white Chevy Impala that Louie said Gustov had their captive stashed in. No Chevy, no Brad. Meeting time for the sisters while Gustov was crying and changing pants in the bathroom.

"If we had more time, Josey could get things out of them even they didn't know they knew." Lydia got nods from her sisters. "But I think we got most of what these weasels know. They both say Brad is in the trunk of a car, a car that isn't here."

Louie was tied again and face down on the bed trying to look inconspicuous. Consuelo had an idea.

"Let's roll. We take the Caddy, start with the streets around the motel, work our way out. We don't spot the car we go back to he hotel and ask Wiola, maybe she can come up with an idea. She always seemed to know just what to do." She looked at her sisters. "We need to take the goons with us."

Lydia was pissed. She wanted to kick the shit out of someone, preferably one of these meatheads who'd been hired to kidnap Brad so MegaDrug, of all people, could pull some big scam. "Let's do it then. Josey, get Laurel and Hardy here ready to travel."

෴

Brad was really scared now. He had lost it a little after the voices left. They probably couldn't hear him kicking the trunk over the sound of the wind and waves.

Someone had obviously driven the car into the water and it had floated along for a short time before stopping. Some water was getting in the trunk for a while there, but it had mostly gone back out. He figured the tide must have been going out because the car had stopped rocking around so much. The air was getting bad so he'd kicked the corner of the trunk for a while and finally got it to bend enough to let a little air in.

There was time to think about things like tides. With a storm coming, the tides were usually a lot higher than normal. He had no idea where he was, but he sure hoped someone got him out of that trunk before the tide came back in.

After an hour of driving deserted streets looking for the white Chevy, they pulled up in front of the hotel.

"I'll try to make this quick." Consuelo let her sisters out, then drove around back for a few things out of the garage. Off she drove into the stormy night with the two men still in the trunk of the Cadillac. She wouldn't tell her sisters what she had in mind, just that she'd given it some thought.

The television was on in the lobby, and Orange Dali was camped out on a sofa with the Weather Channel.

"What's the latest?"

The two women were trying to get their hair under control from all the wind outside. Dali was engrossed and held up a finger.

"Commercial coming!"

Lydia brushed at the owl's nest on her head while Josephine casually ran fingers through her long, silky, shampoo-ad black hair and checked the phone machine for messages. The commercial came on. Dali hit mute but didn't look away from the television, just closed his eyes so he could concentrate.

"Hurricane Zenobia continues to remain stationary. However, forecasters from the National Weather Service expect either a slow northerly or westerly movement by morning with a slight increase in wind speed.

"The quarantine remains in effect at this time. Investigators from the Centers for Disease Control in Atlanta are expected to arrive in Key West tomorrow to check on the possibility that the virus alert is a hoax."

Lydia gave her sister a wink. She'd made a call on the pay phone before they left the motel. The young artist continued his report.

"Two men from a news team feared lost were found alive by the Monroe County Sheriff's Department this evening."

Josephine shook out her now perfect hair and signed she was going to check on Sara and Wiola. Lydia was impressed with Dali's reportage. She'd had him pegged as a bit flighty from seeing him on the street.

"Hey Dali, thanks for filling me in." Still not turning his head, eyes closed, but a big smile now. Proud.

Lydia wondered what Jeremy was up to as she headed for the back still brushing.

* * *

Jeremy was taking a little nap. He must have been tired. He did seem a little winded after the wasps chased him around the backyard.

I found a potato in the trash and rolled it into Jeremy's bathroom while he was conked out on his bed. It was a little big, so I had to use his toothbrush to pack it down into the toilet good and tight. Boy, is he going to be surprised.

Chapter 16

Witchcraft

The wind was gusting like a proud parent at a little league baseball game. The rain squalled when her kid got a bad call, but otherwise kept quiet. By the eighth inning it was a tie game; it could go either way.

When Lydia came into the room, she found Sara sitting up in bed and Wiola in the chair beside her. Josephine was pacing back and forth, stuttering and signing away about Brad and their little adventure at the motel across town.

"So, you didn't find him? What about the two men?"

Wiola's look reminded Lydia of their years as students to a mysterious and often overbearing teacher. Now the teacher was also their real mother.

"Consuelo is dropping them off somewhere, she should be back soon. We're pretty sure they had Brad in the trunk of a car outside of the motel, but we couldn't find the car. We did a lot of looking too."

The hopelessness of the situation was coming down on Lydia and she didn't like it. Wiola had come up with solutions plenty of times in the past, maybe she could help. She obviously understood Brad meant a lot to her, not to mention he was the one person who could clear up the quarantine hoax that was screwing with their new hometown. Wiola looked like she was giving it some thought.

"I guess going to the police wouldn't do much good. They must have plenty to keep them occupied already, not to mention they might not appreciate your little raid on the motel." She frowned a little, but there was mischief in her eyes. She obviously approved of her daughters' initiative.

"Unless you have any better ideas, Wiola, I'm going back out on the streets to look for him when Consuelo gets back with the car. Of course, the gas stations are closed and there isn't much gas left in the tank."

Lydia felt a bad sensation in the pit of her stomach. Wiola and Sara traded a long look. The older woman gestured to her two daughters still standing by the bed to pull some chairs close.

"There is one thing we might try to find your friend. You girls remember Logan and me telling you about lucid dreaming," Wiola looked at Sara again. "We've been doing some catching up while you were gone. A lot of years since we've seen each other. Sara here always had a lot of vivid dreams when she was a child, and she had some expert instruction in lucid dreaming when we were in that house in Mexico. Anyway, from what she's told me here today, it sounds like your big sister is quite the accomplished dreamer these days. Even more so than I had hoped."

An approving nod at Sara.

"I told you girls before that meditation, lucid dreaming, and remote viewing were all related. A lot of things in the sorcerer's world are just lucid dreaming in one form or another. When Rosa told you to try to find Sara, it wasn't just so you'd find out about your real mother, there was another reason too."

Wiola took a long breath and looked at each of her daughters before continuing.

"Each of you has certain unique abilities that Logan and I recognized and helped you develop, and over the years you've grown into independent and strong women.

"But there is a strength and power that comes with a group that is unlike anything we can do individually. As you know, in the sorcerer's world four is a very strong number — the four winds, the four directions of the compass. Rosa knew Logan and I had trained you not only to be able to deal with the world of men and machines, but also to someday, the four of you, be able to go into dreaming as one. There is so much power there if you want to catch a ride on it.

"I had hoped we could work into it slowly, someday after you were all together again. Teach you girls how to dream as one so you could access worlds the sorcerers of antiquity experienced. Maybe take your dear old mom along." A smile and a wink. "But if we're going to try to use dreaming to find your friend, we're going to have to go with what we have now and hope for the best."

∽

Brad wasn't doing too good. He'd been shot with a stun-gun, trussed-up, and left on a hard tile floor; had run for his life through the streets of Key West; almost had his knee knocked off with a car door; was jammed in a car trunk and then banged around by waves. The waves weren't as bad with the tide going out, and he finally gave in to his body's desperate need for sleep. His troubled dreams were of giant squid with guns.

☙

Lydia went across the street to Brad's house while Josephine worked on a sleeping potion that Wiola had started her on.

"The more I think about this, the more it seems like one of my poorer ideas."

Wiola was having second thoughts. It was a tricky maneuver at best, and that's with real dreamers in top form. The only real dreamer she had was lying in front of her and looked like a famine relief poster child.

"Don't worry, Mom, the girls are pretty tough. If we can get them into dreaming, I'm sure they'll give it their best shot." Sara had just finished another bowl of the soup Josephine had made following her oldest sister's instructions.

"We'll know soon enough, I guess. As soon as Consuelo gets back we'll get everyone together for a rehearsal. You sure you're feeling up to this, Sara?"

As if on cue, Sara let loose a good belch and a grin. "Wouldn't miss it for the world!"

The front door slammed and Consuelo headed for Sara's room. "No sign of the white Chevy and the car's almost out of gas. How's it going, Sara, ready to do some alligator wrestling yet?"

She got smiles from Sara and Wiola. Consuelo knew those smiles. Dead-serious smiles. Something was up. She changed gears.

"Okay. What's the plan?"

∞

Wiola had told Lydia to go to Brad's house and "drink in his essence." Whatever. She just felt like shit she couldn't do anything for the man she'd fallen for so hard when he was in serious trouble. The fact that he'd gotten snatched out of her hotel while trying to help pretty much sucked as well. Usually when she thought about Brad, she ended up dwelling on the gay thing. That seemed so trivial now.

She lay on Brad's bed and stuck her face in his pillow. The next thing she knew Wiola was there by the bed.

"Come on honey, it's time."

Lydia was a little groggy so Wiola hooked their arms together and led her back across the street. The three other women were standing in the darkened lobby huddled together holding on to one another. Wiola brought her to the waiting sisters who then formed a circle holding hands, with Wiola in the center.

"Remember, if you're alone and want to change dreams, or feel yourself starting to wake too soon, spin like this and say to yourself where you want to go and that you are dreaming. It will seem much too real to be a dream; so keep reminding yourself, or you'll wake up or slip into a regular dream." Wiola started spinning inside the circle with her arms out, but only for a few seconds. "When you're in a group and dreaming together, you can't break contact with the others. To change dreams you must rub your hands together like this." She held her elbows out and started rubbing her hands together slowly. Wiola's eyes were wild, and she looked more like a sorceress than her daughters had ever seen her. The woman was witch to the bone.

"Lock your arms together and rub! Tell yourself this is a lucid dream, and hold your thoughts to your task!" All five women rubbed their hands in unison, faster and faster. "Not too fast! Remember we want to find —"

Lydia felt a little dizzy while rubbing her hands together, but she seemed to wake up the rest of the way from her nap as soon as she stopped. It had gotten darker and she wondered where everyone else had gone without her noticing. She went to the back looking for them.

Consuelo slipped out the front door and walked down the dark empty streets of Key West. There was light upstairs at the rooftop clothing-optional bar, a place she had been to only briefly once before.

She sipped a beer and relaxed looking over Duval Street while a body-paint artist drew a butterfly that covered her entire chest. He was a really cute guy and his brush seemed to be paying particular attention to her nipples.

Josephine went back to her room to wait for Wiola. She'd planned to check on the sleeping potion in her lab, but forgot about it when she saw her little Ben lying on the bed.

"Josephine, my love, I have something new we can try in the hangover cure."

This sounded good to her. She hoped it was a mango, since the sight of her diminutive lover on the bed was giving her ideas.

"Here it is, under the bed, Josephine. Give me a hand with it." She reached under the bed and her fingers touched something mango-smooth, but there was something oily and stringy on it. She got a grip and pulled Jeremy's severed head from under the bed.

Sara started to tell Lydia something, but there was a flicker of shadow across the room that caught her eye. It was Charlie. He must have been following her again, teasing her. The front door was open and she ran out the door after the shadow. She knew where he would go, back to the Indians he had been living with.

She had found the Calusa tribe once before while searching for Charlie. They said they hadn't seen any white man, but there was a wooden carving over the door to their shell mound temple that looked a lot like Charlie. She started to take a short cut to the mound when she remembered, then stopped in her tracks and started spinning with her arms out.

Wiola forgot what she was about to say. That happened a bit more than she'd like to admit these days. She figured it was probably all that peyote when she was younger.

She watched her daughters leave, then went looking for Orange Dali. A powerful gust of wind rattled the window shutters of the old hotel.

There was something she was supposed to do, but Lydia couldn't for the life of her remember what it was. She stopped wandering around the deserted hotel and concentrated. Call someone? Something in the oven? What was it? It hit her so hard she almost fell.

"Brad!"

It was very dark and she couldn't tell where she was. She was lying on her side with her knees to her chest. Someone was lying there with her. She started to reach out her hand and everything bumped hard. Whoever was there with her started moaning.

Toby Smith had been crabbing for a living ever since he almost graduated high school in Key West. Crabbing was damn hard work, but it paid well. Bad part was the closed season. Stone crab season ended just before hurricane season started, and opened back up about the time the big storms were done for the year. Never could see setting out lobster traps for the hurricanes to wash away.

Toby worked alone mostly, lived alone these days too. Had a wife for a while. Married a girl from Islamoranda not long after school, and they settled in Toby's ancestral shack over by the old Navy base. While he was out pulling traps and giving it his all on the water, she was stuck at home or giving it away down at the Navy bar. Wasn't long before she was run off, keeping company with a man driving a beer truck; and Toby was left keeping company with beer, one can at a time.

But that was years ago. He'd made a decent life for himself working his line of crab traps in one of the more prime locations around Key West. Had a good boat with a strong winch on back for pulling the waterlogged wooden traps up from the bottom. The boat didn't have much of a transom at all — the big outboard was mounted mid-ships so he could leave the back open for pulling the heavy traps onboard.

Off-season, Toby was the last one to make money the way his forefathers had. His family had been in the Keys for generations, all the way back to the days of the wreckers.

Those were the days. Toby used to listen to his grandfather tell about how back before there was electricity and lighthouses, Key West was one of the richest cities in the country. Ships from all over the world came to wreck on the coral reefs. Storms would send the ships to their end on the reef, and the wreckers of Key West would race in their boats to be the first to claim the cargo of the doomed merchant ships.

These days there were lighthouses, and all kinds of navigational aids for the ships in the area; but just as sure as God made flotsam, there would still be storms.

So Toby the Crabber became Toby the Wrecker for a few months each year. It was more of a hobby these days, since most people had enough sense not to go out on the water with a hurricane coming. But he'd still find all kinds of plastic buckets, chairs, poles, barbecue grills, metal sheds, and every kind of crap known to man on the little islands after a storm. Sometimes he'd go out in the rough water during the storm if he saw something nice. Found one of those noisy damn jet-ski things washed up once, another time he found most of a flats boat. This was the first time he'd found a car though.

❧

Lydia started to reach her hand out to whoever was moaning, but someone grabbed her hand and pulled hard.

She was standing up and looking into the smiling face of
Sara only inches away. They were outside, near the water.
The wind was blowing her sister's hair.

"Sara!"

"Don't talk! Look around. Remember where we are.
Don't fix your gaze on any one object, just keep your eyes
moving and memorize all you can."

There was some light from a house not far away. Lydia
looked around, and then she was waking up on Brad's bed.

She ran out the door and across the street to the hotel.
Her three sisters were in the lobby and just waking up when
she burst through the door.

"I know where Brad is!"

The other women sprawled over the couches were having a little trouble coming out of it. Consuelo sat up and
rubbed her eyes.

"Where? Is he in Key West?"

"I'm not sure, probably. There was a weird boat with the
motor in the middle and a big pole with a cable to the car. I
was standing on the trunk of a white Chevy, and it was
hanging off the end of this funny boat!" Then she remembered.

"Sara! Sara was there!"

All eyes went to Sara. She looked exhausted.

"It was your dream, Lydia, I was just trying to help
you remember what to do. All I saw was darkness and
you."

"Okay. Let me see, then. The boat was at a little dock,
and there was a house, a tiny house on the shore. And a
man. A man with a pot belly walking to the house from the
boat. He turned and looked at me, and that's when I woke
up!

"We just need to find the man with the funny boat!" Lydia's enthusiasm ebbed when she thought about what she'd said.

"Where's Wiola? And Dali?"

"M-must have gone h-home."

"We need to find this guy with the boat. I'm sure that's where Brad is!"

"Taco B-Bob. M-m-maybe he knows who the m-man is?"

"Yes! Good idea, Josey!" Lydia gave her sister a quick hug. She took a look at Sara. "You better stay here with Sara, get her back to bed. Consuelo?"

"Always ready, Sis! Let's ride!"

They hit the still windy and deserted streets of Key West. Lydia was really wound up in the car.

"What happened with our dreaming? I thought we were going to rehearse?"

Consuelo, driving, shrugged.

"Wiola gave us something to drink to help us sleep, then went to get you. I remember we were all together in the lobby with our arms locked together and she was telling us what to do. I thought it was just the rehearsal. Then I wandered off and ended up in the nude bar. I remember I was having a really good time."

Consuelo made the turn toward the marina with her sister staring at her, hard.

"But it was only a dream, though. Right?"

Consuelo had to think about it a few seconds.

"Sure, a dream. It didn't feel like one at the time though."

☙

After Josephine got a shaky Sara back into bed, she slipped into Jeremy's room and carefully checked the snoring handyman's neck. Only after she was certain everything was attached like it should be did she go to her own room.

∞

There was a faint blue light from a television in Taco Bob's houseboat. His eyes opened as soon as the weight of someone coming aboard make the boat rock just a little different. There was a knock at the door.

∞

"Come in, ladies. Have a seat." Like he was used to getting company in the middle of the night. No problem.

"Hey, Taco Bob, we really hate to bother you so late, but we're looking for someone and it's really important."

A nod for Lydia to continue.

"Okay, so I don't know his name, but he has a boat with a big pole in the back. Kind of a flat boat with the motor in the middle."

"Sounds like a crab or lobster boat. What's the fella look like?"

"I didn't get a good look at his face, but he was thin with a pot belly. Not a real big guy." Lydia realized she needed more. "There was a little house not far from the boat, and I remember now there was a lot of things in the yard, like a junkyard."

"Ah, now we're getting somewhere. There's a fella fancies himself a wrecker over by the Navy base. Name's Toby if I ain't mistaken. Crabs most of the time, got a boat with a big winch on it."

"That must be him!" Lydia looked at her sister, then at their host. "There's one other thing. Our car is just about out of gas and —"

"Come on, we'll take my truck. I wouldn't want you gals going over to Toby's alone anyway. Man's been known to take a shot at strangers from what I've heard."

On the way to Toby's place, Lydia filled Taco Bob in on Brad, the hoods from Miami, and the quarantine hoax. Consuelo sat in the middle, watching the slim, weathered-looking fisherman from the corner of her eye. She did like a man who drove a truck. Then again, she liked a lot of men, no matter what they drove.

"So how did you ladies come to figure your friend Brad was at Toby's place?"

Lydia was hoping he wouldn't ask about that.

"I, uh, saw it in a dream, actually." Then came over in the middle of the night to get you to take us there. Boy, that sounded lame.

"A dream, huh?"

"A special kind of dream. It's like remote viewing through lucid dreaming, you probably never heard of it. I'll explain it to you sometime." This guy had been so nice to them, and he was giving her a really weird look now. He probably thought she was nuts.

"I think this here is the right one. He lives at the end of one of these roads down by the water."

They parked in the overgrown yard near the front of a small tin-roof house. The rain had become a light mist.

"I doubt he heard that horn over the wind if he's over by the water."

There was a truck with its lights on pointed their way out back and more lights off to the side of the truck. They followed a path through the weeds and piles of junk to the back of the house. The truck was backed down to the water, and the boat Lydia had seen was there with a white car hanging off the back. There was a man in the shallow water hooking cable from the truck to the car so he could pull it up on shore. When the man looked up there were three people standing on the dock near his boat.

"Evening, Toby! Nice car! Ladies just want to take a quick look in the trunk of your car here. Don't mean any harm."

Toby stood still in the water and looked at his truck. That let Taco Bob know where the gun was. He eased over so he was between the man in the water and the truck.

"This here is my car! I found her fair and square!"

"Ain't nobody going to try to take your car away, Toby. Just want to look in the trunk real quick, and then we'll leave you be."

There were lights on the boat, and Lydia was looking for something to use on the trunk. Some magician she turned out to be, forgetting her lock picks the one time she really needed them. Consuelo, who'd been keeping a wary eye on the crabber, picked up a long pole with a hook on the end and headed for the back of the car.

"Hold on there! Anything in the trunk is rightfully mine too, you know!"

Lydia turned to the man.

"We think there might be someone in the trunk, a person!"

"Well shit, why didn't you say so in the first place!"

The man waded over to the car and opened the front door. The car was too heavy to get all the way up on the boat, so the front part was still mostly in the water. He found a single key still in the ignition.

"Hold your horses, I got the key right here." He pulled himself up on the boat and gave the key a try in the trunk lock and stepped back.

∞

The light hurt his eyes at first, but he was so happy to see Lydia's face he almost cried.

"Brad!"

Lydia reached in and tried to hug him and pull him out of the trunk at the same time. Consuelo and Toby took his legs, and by the time Taco Bob got on the boat, they had Brad sitting on the deck. He was a little out of it, but smiling even before they got the gag off him.

Consuelo worked freeing his hands and feet while Lydia sat down next to her best friend, put her arms around him, and cried. Things were looking up for Brad. He grabbed Consuelo and hugged both sisters as hard as he could.

"You ladies don't know how glad I am to see you!"

Toby looked over at Taco Bob.

"I reckon this here must be what y'all was looking for then."

Taco Bob gave him a big smile.

"Sure looks like it."

∞

Toby obviously didn't get many visitors and was wound up, wanting to talk.

"I think I seen that blonde gal before, jogging around the island."

Consuelo was trying to check Brad for broken bones while he and Lydia were busy with the hugging and crying thing.

"Don't doubt it, Toby. She's off running miles about everyday. Her and her sisters bought the old Key West Manor Hotel."

"You don't say? You know, that's something all them yankees coming down here got wrong."

"How's that?"

"My granddaddy told me the real deal on that. Said them drunk yankee tourists got so worked up about that fella Hemingway being in Key West, they can't keep a story straight. Not only got it mixed up about what bar he drank at, they got it wrong about the hotel he stayed at when he first came here."

The two sisters were helping a limping Brad walk toward Taco Bob's truck. Consuelo gave a look over her shoulder that said it was time to go.

"Them yankees got it wrong all right, Ol' Papa stayed at the Manor. It was the fella he'd hired to do a portrait was the one staying at the hotel down the street. Granddaddy said the Manor ain't got a widow walk cause a hurricane blowed it off while the crazy painter fella was on it."

"That's mighty interesting, Toby. I got to go, thanks for your help, partner."

"No problem! I gotta tell you the best part, though. Supposed to be some ghost shows up there at the hotel every time there's a hurricane coming. Ain't that rich?"

The old crabber went to laughing and coughing while Taco Bob hurried to catch up with the others. He decided not to tell the sisters about the Hemingway story. They had enough to deal with trying to run that place by themselves. He didn't want to scare them with any stories of ghosts in their hotel.

* * *

My Josephine was so tired, maybe that's why she was looking at me strange. She looked under the bed real carefully and smiled big when she found the ripe mango I'd put there. She said we'd save it for later and hugged me to her chest on the bed. I can take a lot of that kind of treatment.

Chapter 17
Hotel

*The wind kept it up like a tired child who
wouldn't go to sleep. The stars came out
briefly and sang to it. The moon told it a
story. After the sun came in and ran everyone
off, the wind finally calmed down and slept.*

The drive back to the hotel was uneventful as drives in near-hurricane conditions go. It was slow going and a tight fit in the truck with Taco Bob driving, Consuelo next to him, and Lydia and Brad huddled against the far door. Lydia kept fussing over Brad while filling him in on the high points of the quarantine.

Taco Bob wanted to ask Lydia about this dream she'd had. He'd been pretty skeptical, but finding a real, mostly alive biologist in the trunk of the car at Toby's had his curiosity up. Especially since he knew a little about lucid dreaming himself.

But he was too busy at the time to start any serious con-
versations. In spite of the concentration it took to drive
through the wind and rain in the dark, he was very aware of
the young woman pressed against his side. He'd noticed her
quietly looking at him, and when he hit a bump her hand
landed on his leg, and stayed. When her fingertips started
moving in a slow circular motion he had to remove the hand
or end up in a ditch.

"Uh, Consuelo, I'm trying to drive here. Maybe you
could try the radio, find us some news on this storm."

"Sure"

There was plenty of static, excited voices talking fast in
Spanish, music, and finally a CNN weather update from a
Miami station. The news was good. Hurricane Zenobia was
turning west, away from Florida. The forecasters had it losing strength crossing the Gulf of Mexico, then hitting a
sparsely populated area just south of Brownsville, Texas.

They decided the best way to get things straightened out
was for Brad to go to the airport and meet the CDC people
from Atlanta. Since they still had some time until the plane
was due, they'd have Taco Bob drop them at the hotel so
they could re-group in the lobby and tell Brad the rest of the
story.

"I'm pretty impressed with the way you ladies handled
those two hoods. Just what did you do with them, Consuelo?"

Consuelo got into telling the tale. This made driving easier for Taco Bob.

"I took the fancy dresser, Louie, out to the sewage treatment plant. Held him up over the rankest tank and told him

to tell me why he shouldn't get tied off in there for a few hours. Started telling me all kinds of stuff about his partner, who at the time had the spacious Caddy trunk all to himself. He starts telling me about Gustov poisoning the birds at the beach with rat poison. Tells me he thinks the big tough guy is afraid of birds and won't admit it. I get an idea. I stop by their little motel room real quick since it's on the way.

"You ever hear the story about that parking lot at Searstown? Supposedly, that area was a popular marsh spot for the seabirds for like, forever. They paved it over for the lot, and generations of birds keep coming back there anyway. Something in their genes I guess.

"Anyway, I got some big nails and rope out of the toolbox. Hammered the nails down in the asphalt and tied dear Gus out there spread eagle. Mashed up two big bags of corn chips I'd grabbed out of their room and sprinkled him really good. I kept the gag in his mouth so he wouldn't scare the birds while they pecked." Consuelo looked pleased with herself.

"So what did you do with Louie then?"

"Oh, I tied him off in the sewage tank anyway. His screams made a really cool echo in the wind. Anyway, it'll be getting light out before long, so I imagine they'll both be found in a few hours. I doubt we'll be hearing any more from them though. From what we learned about their boss, they'll most likely be in a hurry to get out of town, the state, and probably the country."

Brad looked relieved to hear this.

☙

When Taco Bob stopped the truck in front of the hotel, there was an ambulance parked in the dark just down the street. Lydia looked at her sister.

"Where'd that ambulance come from?"

"Beats me."

Brad reached over and shook hands with Taco Bob. "Thanks so much for your help."

"Hey, no problem. Glad to do it."

Brad got out with Lydia.

"Thanks, Taco Bob. You'll have to come by for dinner sometime." She was holding Brad's hand, heading for the front door of the hotel. "Consuelo, be a dear and give him a hug for me, will you?"

Taco Bob stiffened as Consuelo threw her arms around him. He expected a bone-crusher, but got the softest, most sensuous embrace of his life. Two bright eyes looked up out of the blonde hair.

"Thanks, Taco Bob." Consuelo scooted across the seat and was out the door, giving a little wave as she headed for the hotel. "See you soon!"

Taco Bob watched her slip into the hotel, then shook himself out and took it on home.

When she opened the front door of the hotel, Consuelo was thinking about asking Taco Bob to take her fishing sometime and wondering if he had a girlfriend. She almost rear-ended Brad and Lydia standing just inside.

"No one moves, or the skinny one gets it!"

Everyone was staring at the wired, dumpy-looking guy standing there with a gun pointed at Sara. She was sitting on a couch in the lobby next to a very unhappy

Josephine. Brad and Lydia not moving in front of her. Wait for a diversion from one of her sisters? Or do a roll, come up and launch off the other couch, make a grab for the gun and the guy's eyes? Oh well, no time like the present.

Consuelo was about to spring when the guy fired a shot just over Brad's head.

"You! Blondie! On the floor! Sit on your hands! Now!"

So much for that plan. Guy was twitching around like a speed freak. Better do what the jerk says, don't want to get somebody shot. Just sit and remember the training. Patience.

"That's a good girl! You two, on the couch here! Blondie stays on the floor, scoot up against the wall, little girl."

Eyes on this guy are crazy. There, he's sniffing like he's been doing coke.

"That's good, Blondie. You're a cute little thing, but I got a feeling you were about to do something very bad there a minute ago. I want —"

"What's going on here?"

Lydia sitting on the couch interrupted the jerk. Four people on the couch. Brad looked confused, Lydia and Josey looked pissed, Sara looked sick. This sucked.

Guy turned and pointed the gun, looked like a 45, at Lydia.

"You, shut your mouth! I got the gun, which means I'm in charge here. Understand?" Guy was sure wired, kept sweeping the gun at everyone, especially Consuelo. "And I want some straight answers here, no more of this stuttering or 'I don't know' bullshit I been getting from these two." The eyes on the couch had all gone to highly pissed. "First question: Is this Dr. Brad Mulberry?"

A door slammed in back of the hotel and Jeremy came in the lobby looking at a horse racing program and scratching his belly.

"Hey, has anyone seen my ... Oops."

"On the floor, fatso! Now! Face down, arms out!"

Consuelo started coming off the floor when the gun swung back her way. Guy definitely looked like he would put a bullet in her head. Back down. Patience.

Joey Two Thumbs was not enjoying his trip to Key West. Things had been going so well back in Miami. Nice little job for the drug company had come at a good time. One of his main sources of income — shaking down crooked politicians and lobbyists — was in serious decline since some hot-shot newspaper columnist/novelist had too many of the politicians in Miami playing nice. Used to be you could hardly swing a dead cat in that town without hitting at least a commissioner on the take.

The first draw on payment from the drug company had just been made the way he liked it — on time and in cash. And there was a little bonus with the payment. Some pills and powder that went really well with twelve-year-old single malt Scotch. A couple of class whores to complete the night's entertainment were on their way. Then the phone rang.

The big moron who worked for Joey said he might have a problem, then hung up. Finally got somebody to answer the fucking phone at the motel. Offered money and then a pistol whipping, but the guy wouldn't go check on the room. Asswipe at the motel just knew no one could get in or out of Key West, so he got with the smart mouth. Guy hadn't planned on Joey Thumbs.

Guy about shit when Joey walked in the motel office a few hours later. A couple of shots with the 45 into the guy's computer made sure there wasn't going to be any more smart mouth. Told everything he knew then, which wasn't much. Just that Gus and Louie might have left with three young women he recognized as the new owners of the Key West Manor Hotel. Joey was pretty wound up after the ride down through the Keys, so he slapped the motel guy around anyway, just to work off some stress. Hey, just because your world is going to shit is no reason not to be concerned with your health. He planned to relieve a lot more stress when he found Gus and Louie.

So then he'd driven the ambulance over to the hotel. Ambulance was a stroke of luck. Drove the Caddy down through the Keys trying to figure how he was going to get through the fucking quarantine roadblock when he got to Key West. Pulled over along the road to take a piss and here comes the answer. Step out in the road, get your hands up waving around, and if you have a chrome 45, you get a free ambulance complete with driver. This one even came with a patient zonked out in back, a big one. Got right through the stupid roadblock, no problemo. Actually, things had gone fairly smooth, up until these little broads decided to be a pain in the ass.

"So is this Dr. Brad Mulberry or not? Don't be fucking me around here, people. My doctor says I need to take it easy on the stress, so if you don't cooperate here, I may just have to shoot someone. Fuck it, I think I will anyway."

A quick pinch of that fine powder for each nostril, then draw a bead on the little blond. Somebody's coming in the door. Now what?

"What the fuck do you want?"

Joey couldn't believe it. The fucking ambulance driver and patient. Jesus H. Fucking Christ but that patient is big. Driver had a big lump on his forehead.

"I really hate to bother you folks, you're obviously mighty busy and all. I was just hoping we could get the keys back to our ambulance parked out front."

Joey couldn't believe this shit.

"Fuck no you can't have the keys! And who the fuck are you anyway? I see you here in the light, you got the right uniform, but you don't look like no ambulance driver to me!"

"Name's George, and this here mountain of a man is my partner, Lenny. Folks like to call us the Dalton Gang."

George Dalton wasn't having one of his better trips to Key West. Things had started off well enough, all the excitement with the hurricane coming had been the perfect opportunity for him and his partner to practice their specialty: prison escape.

In their long and storied careers in crime, the Daltons always seemed to supplement their inevitable felonious shortcoming with generous amounts of bad luck. Which gave them ample time in closed environments with a segment of society where escape strategies are almost a religion. It turned out to be the one thing they were good at, amazingly good at.

On the way from Miami's Krome Avenue Correctional to Homestead, George had an idea. Earlier they'd dropped the prison shrink off in the swamps and taken his clothes and car. Hurricane news on the radio gave George the idea. They started looking for a fire station.

Since Lenny was more than just a few bricks shy of a load, George had always tried to take care of his childlike but formidable partner. In a business where size quite often did matter, George would usually let the big man take care of things like politely tying up paramedics and firefighters while he checked out their clothes lockers. He selected a spiffy uniform for himself and a nice shiny red and blue ambulance for the drive down to Key West to settle an old score. The only thing they could find close to Lenny's size was a hospital gown.

"This sure is a swell ride we got, George! Can you turn on the siren again? Please, George?"

"I told you we only turn that on for emergencies! Like when that old lady pulled out in front of us back in Key Largo!"

"Yeah! Boy, that was some fun, huh, George? I shore hope she can swim! When we going to eat? I shore am hungry, George."

Everything was going great, except there weren't any restaurants open as they were driving down through the Keys, so Lenny ate all the drugs in the ambulance instead. George couldn't believe it.

Then the big lummox says he don't feel so good and finally ends up in back passed out. Then there's this guy standing in the road. Pretty embarrassing for a couple of hardened criminals to get car-jacked.

After they got through the roadblock at the Key West bridge, the crazy car-jack fucker has him pull over, whacks him with a big gun, rolls a still unconscious Lenny out the back, and takes off with their ambulance. This sucked mightily, since the ambulance was an important part of George's plan to kill a certain somebody. They'd tried about everything in the past, from machine guns to rockets, but this was proving to be a hard man to kill.

The game plan this time was serious stuff. They weren't screwing around, no sir. Once in Key West, they planned to go straight to the Navy Base and see if they couldn't find a nice nuclear warhead that would fit in the back of the ambulance. Then go find Taco Bob, tie him to the bomb, and blow the fucker up but good. There were some details that needed to be worked out on his plan, but George figured if you were going to be a successful criminal you had to learn to think on your feet.

But walking around Key West in the rain and wind looking for their ambulance was definitely not part of the plan. At least Lenny had sobered up some, and they'd found their ride outside this hotel; but now it looked like he was about to get shot by this crazy car-jacker.

"Really, mister. We don't mean no harm, at least to nobody here. You just hand over the keys to our ambulance, and we'll be on our way."

"Fuck that! You two beat it. Now!"

George motioned to his towering partner.

"Lenny here is mighty cranky since he ain't had nothing to eat today but drugs. You folks ever hear of us, or what this man does when he's cranky?" Everyone shook their head no, except the little man on the floor who just stared with his mouth open. "Nobody heard of us? Shit. Well, Lenny, kill that couch." The big man reached over and grabbed the empty couch next to the little blond on the floor, picked it up off the ground and ripped it in half.

Everyone stared in disbelief. Except the man with the big silver gun, who turned and shot George in the chest.

❧

Lenny was having a great time in Key West. Escaping always gave him an even better appetite than usual, but all those drugs made him forget about being hungry, at least for a while. He'd never been so high before, since George usually didn't let him take drugs in prison because they were bad for you, and because they could be traded for good healthy stuff like cigarettes and porn.

All those lights were sure fun to look at though as they drove along in the ambulance. Lenny was so happy he'd tried to give his best friend a hug.

"Get off me you big ape, I'm trying to drive here!"

"You're my best friend in the whole world, George!"

"Jeez, Lenny, you're acting even weirder than usual! What were you doing in back anyhow? You didn't get into the drugs did you?"

"Just the ones in the locked cabinet. I think I don't feel so good, George."

"Not in here, you big dummy!"

That was the best part for Lenny. After he got done puking in Technicolor, he found a little land crab there alongside the road. He'd had it in his pocket ever since. It was his little secret from George.

While they walked around Key West in the rain looking for their ambulance, Lenny would slip a hand in his pocket and pet the crab. That was some kind of good, but now George had done gone and got himself shot.

"George!"

Lenny jumped in the way of any more bullets and picked up his partner. He stood there with tears streaming down his face.

"No! You can't shoot George! Speak to me, George!"

There was some commotion behind him and the big man saw the little blonde woman pulling the gun away from the car-jacker while kicking him in the face. Still bawling and holding his best friend with one arm, Lenny reached over and grabbed the bad man by the head, then flipped him through the front window of the hotel.

"Speak to me, George! You can't die, George, we still ain't ate yet!"

George made a muffled sound Lenny could barely hear.

"Let go of me you big goon! I got a bullet-proof vest with the ambulance uniform!"

When George stepped back he was a little shaky and holding his chest, but much to Lenny's relief, he wasn't dead. The big man's tears of anguish turned to tears of joy. He bet they even had something to make a sandwich with right here at the hotel. Lenny was having a great time in Key West.

"Consuelo, keep the gun on him!"

Lydia ran out the front door and checked on the crazy bastard lying in the broken window glass in front of the hotel. Josephine pulled on some gloves and gave the unconscious man a quick check right there on the sidewalk. Lydia got the sign that he was out but mostly okay. Some cuts from the window and probably a concussion. Consuelo relaxed, but stood ready. Lydia was not happy.

"Who the hell is this guy anyway?"

Sara came to the window. "From what he said before you got here, it sounds like he's the boss of the guys who kidnapped Brad."

Jeremy came outside and started going through the prone mobster's pockets. Lydia saw him try to put something in his own pockets.

"Put it on the ground, Jeremy."

Jeremy looked up and saw what must be his worst nightmare. Consuelo with a pissed look and a big gun, both aimed his way.

The two guys from the ambulance came outside. The big goofy one sniffling with a big smile, the little one with the shifty eyes still rubbing his chest.

"If y'all be so kind as to give us those keys to our ambulance, we'll be on our way."

Lydia was ready for fewer people.

"Sure, here." She looked at Consuelo to check out her own suspicions, and got the sign these guys were dirty, but probably not a threat to them.

"What are you two up to, anyway?"

"Oh, we were just in the area, thought we'd do a little sightseeing around the Navy base, then maybe look up an old acquaintance."

Jeremy had stopped going through pockets and was just staring up at the two men. The big one cleared his throat.

"I don't supposed y'all got some baloney and bread I could make a sandwich with?"

Lydia looked at the gangster laying on the sidewalk and had an idea.

"Consuelo, why don't you whip up a couple of your famous sandwiches real quick."

Consuelo handed the gun over to her older sister and disappeared into the kitchen.

"Since you boys have an ambulance already, I don't suppose you could —," Lydia pointed the gun towards the man on the ground.

The little man called George started to say something about needing to leave when the big one picked up the mobster like a sack of potatoes and held him under his arm. His eyes never left the door Consuelo had gone through.

A few minutes later Brad and Lydia watched the strange men called the Daltons walking toward the ambulance. The big one still had the mobster under his arm but was so busy working on his sandwich, he didn't seem to notice the unconscious man's head banging into lampposts and parking meters along the way.

With Brad standing conveniently next to her, Lydia decided it was time for a hug.

"Thank goodness they're gone. We still need to get you over to the airport to meet the CDC people."

"Right. I should get cleaned up a little first and maybe use your phone. I have a friend over at the Navy base. I'll let him know they might have a couple of odd characters coming to visit."

The sisters decided to make a call to Detroit while Brad was in the shower. The man who had spent a few days in their basement in Pine Cove was humbled and horrified to hear from them. He agreed it would be an honor for him to visit a certain CEO again and deliver a simple message in a memorable way.

Brad was feeling much better by the time Josephine checked him over. He was pronounced bruised but unbro-

ken. Sara was formally introduced to Brad. She suggested
he eat plenty of soup to get his strength back and then went
back to bed. The sisters fed him and fussed over him, especially Lydia.

"I still don't understand how you knew that crabber had
found the car though."

Lydia wished people would quit asking this.

"Maybe we'll let you ask our mother about that. She
seems to have left, but she might be able to explain it better
than me." Lydia threw the mother thing in there to change
the subject. She remembered the strange look from Taco
Bob when she'd mentioned lucid dreaming and remote
viewing.

"Your mother?" Brad looked at the three women sitting
with him. "I thought you told me your mother died. A year
ago. In California."

"Well, she did. But this is our real mother. She was one
of the teachers we told you about, and she's living here in
Key West. Hangs out with that street artist Orange Dali."

Brad was looking confused.

"Anyway, I'm sure she would love to tell you all about
it." Lydia decided she needed to try to keep her mother
away from Brad. She'd explain it to him someday herself.
Someday.

Brad looked at the clock behind the front desk. The sun
would be up soon.

"I better get to the airport. I want to be there when those
people from the CDC get off the plane."

Consuelo jumped up and ran out the back. Josephine
was about to nod out on the couch. Lydia patted her on the
shoulder.

"You better get some sleep, Josey. Consuelo and I will get Brad to the airport." Brad stood up to receive Josephine's sleepy hug before she dragged off to bed.

"Goodnight, Josephine, thanks again for everything!"

Josephine gave a little wave over her shoulder as she left the room. Lydia stood and hit the remote to turn off the television. They were alone. Brad took Lydia's hands in his.

"I really do want to know how you knew that crabber had the car." He put his finger to her lips before she could say anything. "But you don't have to tell me now." He gave her a quick wink and a smile.

Lydia got lost a little in that smile and went for the clinch. She hugged him, trying not to cry.

"Okay, I'll try to explain it someday." But she had her face buried in his chest and it sounded more like. "Mumft, mm mum mmft mumftmm."

Lydia got a grip and looked up straight into those gorgeous eyes. Her lips were quivering just a tiny bit as he brought his mouth slowly to hers. As their lips barely touched, Consuelo brought the Caddy to a screeching stop outside the front door and laid on the horn.

"Let's go, folks! We haven't got a lot of gas here, you know!"

The horn made them jump, but they held on to each other for another few seconds. Lydia was pissed, but grinning. "That counts as a kiss, you know!"

Brad laughed, "Whatever you say, my dear. I believe our carriage awaits."

And they walked out the front door of the Key West Manor Hotel, arm-in-arm.

* * *

A week later the hotel was completely booked.
My Josephine and her sisters were happy to be
so busy. Things were getting back to normal.

The town was again under siege from wave
after wave of eager tourists looking for a taste
of the Key West Experience and a clever T-shirt
to show the neighbors back home. Rental
scooters buzzed the streets, maneuvering
around delivery trucks and barefoot locals.
Music blared from bars and parrots squawked
from porches.

Details of the Key West Nile Virus hoax were
sketchy at best, and that left plenty of room for
speculation. But after a few days, even the
most eloquent and persistent of the local
practicing barstool theorists had found
something else to expound upon. Soon it was
just another vague story in a town known for
fuzzy memories.

The sisters did some checking and learned
MegaDrug had moved quickly and would
eventually close on several lucrative real estate
transactions. But the net result had to be far
short of original expectations. This was, of
course, due to the reappearance of the missing
biologist and the subsequent early lifting of the
quarantine.

A couple of days after that happened,
MegaDrug's CEO, some old guy named
Greenfield, ordered all plans for future
drugstores in South Florida scrapped. The
inside story is he once again woke up with a
large-caliber handgun stuck in his mouth.
Supposedly for health reasons, he soon
afterward moved to an undisclosed island in
the South Pacific.

Poor Wiola never did find Dali. She told
Josephine her last blurry memory of the dream
was a fleeting shadow flowing up the stairs of
the hotel. She went after it, thinking it must be
her Dali wanting a better look at the storm. She
couldn't remember anything after that, though,
and woke up in her own bed the next morning.
At first she planned to get everyone to dream
together again to find him, but then she
thought better of it. She was pretty sad. She
said perhaps her attempts to tame the wild
artist had been a little too much and he'd taken
the opportunity to move on. I think she's
getting over it. Wiola may have lost a lover, but
she isn't hurting for daughters these days.

Sara gets stronger every day. She's staying here
at the hotel, helping her sisters. Wiola told her
that working with people at the hotel might be
the best thing for her. Deal with sunburned
vacationers from Pittsburgh for a while instead
of vaporous phantoms from other dimensions.
Sara agreed.

That fisherman guy, Taco Bob, helped Sara sell some of her gold at the best price so she could invest in mutual funds and a red convertible. She went on a date even, a real date. Some weird guy called Fish Daddy with a bird on his head took her to dinner at Blue Heaven last Friday night. Sara says she always did like older men.

They didn't know it, but I heard the man wearing the expensive linen suit with the slight water stains sitting next to them in the restaurant that night was Toby Smith. He'd found the suit in a suitcase in the back seat of the Chevy. It was a little tight around the middle, but otherwise a perfect fit.

Consuelo is learning body painting from some guy she met a few days ago at that rooftop nude bar on Duval. I heard her say she's also trying to get Taco Bob to take her fishing sometime.

The media forgot about Brad after a couple of days. He just told them what he told the police and told the truth, up to a point. He said he'd never gotten a good look at the two men who held him in the motel room, and he'd slipped away when they both went out of the room. The police probably wouldn't fully appreciate the little party the sisters threw for his captors, so he left that part out. He didn't mention the part about being stuffed in a car trunk and ending up as catch-of-the-day for a local crabber either. No one ever did figure out how the car had gotten from the motel parking lot to the water anyway.

Supposedly the police searched the room at the motel, but someone had gotten there first and thoroughly cleaned it. Nobody ever heard what happened to the two hoods or their crazy boss. The two guys with the ambulance turned out to be escaped convicts. They were arrested at the Navy base trying to steal a sophisticated piece of machinery that looked like a bomb but turned out to be a high-tech trash compactor.

The police finally lost interest in Brad. Lydia didn't. She and Brad are getting closer, not close in the way Lydia would like, but closer nonetheless.

Brad came by late this afternoon to pick Lydia up for a ride up the Keys on his motorcycle. Afterwards they were going to check out the latest hot new Marty Manatee impersonator at Sloppy Joes. Lydia was looking through the mail when he came in and struck one of his better dramatic poses.

"There's a lotta road out there, and it's calling my name!"

Lydia rolled her eyes and smiled.

"Be right with you, my dashing vagabond." She was reading. "Check this out. Here's a letter from a real estate agent representing Jack's Drugs. They say Jack's wants to buy our hotel." She shook her head and dropped the letter in the trash.

"I think we already did this. Let's go see the sunset from the highest bridge in the Keys at sixty miles an hour instead."

So Josephine is at the front desk this evening. When she's not working in the hotel, she and I are putting in some long hours on her hangover cure. We need to find a new test subject though. Jeremy saw me rolling a mango through the hotel last night and quit his job. Actually, he didn't see me, just the mango. Rolling along.

Said he wasn't going to work in a haunted hotel. Lydia told him it was probably just a side effect from all the hangover potions he's been drinking, but he quit anyway.

I'm not worried though — he'll be back.

Acknowledgments

Thanks to Annie and Sandra for once again showing me the errors of my ways. Thanks also to Sara Leigh, Eva, and Alan S.

A special thank you to my family and friends for all the encouragement and advice along the way.

Robert Tacoma lives in central Florida and is the author of Key Weird and Key Wierder.